THE MANTLE AND OTHER STORIES

BY

NIKOLAI GOGOL

TRANSLATED BY CLAUD FIELD

AND WITH AN INTRODUCTION ON GOGOL
BY
PROSPER MERIMÉE

British Library Cataloguing-in-Publication Data
A catalogue record for this book is available from the
British Library

Contents

Nikolai Gogol

Nikolai Vasilievich Gogol was born in Sorochintsi, Ukraine in 1809. He attended the Poltava boarding school, and then the Nehzin high school, where he wrote for the school's literary journal and acted in theatrical productions. In 1828, after leaving school, Gogol moved to St. Petersburg with the ambition of becoming a professional author. At his own expense, he published a long Romantic poem. It was universally derided, and Gogol bought and destroyed all the copies, swearing never to write poetry again.

In 1831, Gogol brought out the first volume of his Ukrainian stories, *Evenings on a Farm Near Dikanka*. It met with immediate success, and he followed it a year later with a second volume. Around this time, Gogol met the great Russian poet Aleksandr Pushkin, with whom he developed a close friendship. Over the next decade or so, he worked with great industry, producing a great amount of short stories. Of these, 'The Nose' is regarded as a masterwork of comic short fiction, and 'The Overcoat' is now seen as one of the greatest short stories ever written; some years later, Dostoyevsky famously stated "We all come out from Gogol's 'Overcoat'." He also published *Dead Souls* (1842), a satirisation of serfdom, seen by many critics as the first 'modern' Russian novel and his greatest longer work.

Gogol spent time living abroad in later life, settling in Rome and developing a passion for opera. As he got older, criticism of his work began to drain him, and he turned to religion, making a pilgrimage to Jerusalem in 1848. Upon his return to Russia, under the encouragement of the fanatical priest, Father Konstantinovskii, Gogol subjected himself to a fatal course of fasting. He died in Moscow in 1852, aged 42. He is seen by many contemporary critics as one of the greatest short story writers who has ever lived, and the Father of Russia's Golden Age of Realism.

PREFACE

As a novel-writer and a dramatist, Gogol appears to me to deserve a minute study, and if the knowledge of Russian were more widely spread, he could not fail to obtain in Europe a reputation equal to that of the best English humorists.

A delicate and close observer, quick to detect the absurd, bold in exposing, but inclined to push his fun too far, Gogol is in the first place a very lively satirist. He is merciless towards fools and rascals, but he has only one weapon at his disposal—irony. This is a weapon which is too severe to use against the merely absurd, and on the other hand it is not sharp enough for the punishment of crime; and it is against crime that Gogol too often uses it. His comic vein is always too near the farcical, and his mirth is hardly contagious. If sometimes he makes his reader laugh, he still leaves in his mind a feeling of bitterness and indignation; his satires do not avenge society, they only make it angry.

As a painter of manners, Gogol excels in familiar scenes. He is akin to Teniers and Callot. We feel as though we had seen and lived with his characters, for he shows us their eccentricities, their nervous habits, their slightest gestures. One lisps, another mispronounces his words, and a third hisses because he has lost a front tooth. Unfortunately Gogol is so absorbed in this minute study of details that he too often forgets to subordinate them to the main action of the story. To tell the truth, there is no ordered plan in his works, and—a strange trait in an author who sets up as a realist—he takes no care to preserve an atmosphere of probability. His most carefully painted scenes are clumsily connected—they begin and end abruptly; often the author's great carelessness in construction destroys, as though wantonly, the illusion produced by the truth of his descriptions and the naturalness of his conversations.

The immortal master of this school of desultory but ingenious and attractive story-tellers, among whom Gogol is entitled to a high place, is Rabelais, who cannot be too much admired and studied, but to imitate whom nowadays would, I think, be dangerous and difficult. In spite of the indefinable grace of his obsolete language, one can hardly read twenty pages of Rabelais in succession. One soon wearies of this eloquence, so original and so eloquent, but the drift of which escapes every reader except some Œdipuses like Le Duchat or Éloi Johanneau. Just as the observation of animalculæ under the microscope fatigues the eye, so does the perusal of these brilliant pages tire the mind. Possibly not a word of them is superfluous, but possibly also they might be entirely eliminated from the work of which they form part, without sensibly detracting from its merit. The art of choosing among the innumerable details which nature offers us is, after all, much more difficult than that of observing them with attention and recording them with exactitude.

The Russian language, which is, as far as I can judge, the richest of all the European family, seems admirably adapted to express the most delicate shades of thought. Possessed of a marvellous conciseness and clearness, it can with a single word call up several ideas, to express which in another tongue whole phrases would be necessary. French, assisted by Greek and Latin, calling to its aid all its northern and southern dialects—the language of Rabelais, in fact, is the only one which can convey any idea of this suppleness and this energy. One can imagine that such an admirable instrument may exercise a considerable influence on the mind of a writer who is capable of handling it. He naturally takes delight in the picturesqueness of its expressions, just as a draughtsman with skill and a good pencil will trace delicate contours. An excellent gift, no doubt, but there are few things which have not their disadvantages. Elaborate execution is a considerable merit if it is reserved for the chief parts of a work; but if it is uniformly lavished on all the accessory parts also, the whole produces, I fear, a monotonous effect.

I have said that satire is, in my opinion, the special characteristic of Gogol's talent: he does not see men or things in a bright light. That does not mean that he is an unfaithful observer, but his descriptions betray a certain preference for the ugly and the sad elements in life. Doubtless these two disagreeable elements are only too easily found, and it is precisely for that reason that they should not be investigated with insatiable curiosity. We would form a terrible idea of Russia—of "Holy Russia," as her children call her—if we only judged her by the pictures which Gogol draws. His characters are almost entirely confined to idiots, or scoundrels who deserve to be hung. It is a well-known defect of satirists to see everywhere the game which they are hunting, and they should not be taken too literally. Aristophanes vainly employed his brilliant genius in blackening his contemporaries; he cannot prevent us loving the Athens of Pericles.

Gogol generally goes to the country districts for his characters, imitating in this respect Balzac, whose writings have undoubtedly influenced him. The modern facility of communication in Europe has brought about, among the higher classes of all countries and the inhabitants of the great cities, a conventional uniformity of manners and customs, e.g. the dress-coat and round hat. It is among the middle classes remote from great towns that we must look to-day for national characteristics and for original characters. In the country, people still maintain primitive habits and prejudices—things which become rarer from day to day. The Russian country gentlemen, who only journey to St Petersburg once in a lifetime, and who, living on their estates all the year round, eat much, read little and hardly think at all—these are the types to which Gogol is partial, or rather which he pursues with his jests and sarcasms. Some critics, I am told, reproach him for displaying a kind of provincial patriotism. As a Little Russian, he is said to have a predilection for Little Russia over the rest of the Empire. For my own part, I find him impartial enough or even too general in his criticisms, and on the other hand too severe on anyone whom he places under the microscope of his observation. Pushkin was accused, quite wrongly in my opinion, of scepticism, immorality, and of belonging to the Satanic school; however he discovered in an old country manor his admirable Tatiana. One regrets that Gogol has not been equally fortunate.

I do not know the dates of Gogol's different works, but I should be inclined to believe that his short stories were the first in order of publication. They seem to me to witness to a certain vagueness in the author's mind, as though he were making experiments in order to ascertain to what style of work his genius was best adapted. He has produced an historical romance inspired by the perusal of Sir Walter Scott, fantastic legends, psychological studies, marked by a mixture of sentimentality and grotesqueness. If my conjecture is correct, he has been obliged to ask himself for some time whether he should take as his model Sterne, Walter Scott, Chamisso, or Hoffmann. Later on he has done better in following the path which he has himself traced out. "Taras Bulba," his historical romance, is an animated and, as far as I know, correct picture of the Zaporogues, that singular people whom Voltaire briefly mentions in his "Life of Charles XII." In the sixteenth and seventeenth centuries the Zaporogues played a great part in the annals of Russia and of Poland; they then formed a republic of soldiers, or rather of filibusters, established on the islands of the Don, nominal subjects sometimes of the Kings of Poland, sometimes of the Grand Dukes of Moscow, sometimes even of the Ottoman Porte. At bottom they were extremely independent bandits, and ravaged their neighbours' territory with great impartiality. They did not allow women to live in their towns, which were a kind of nomad encampments; it was there that the Cossack aspirants to military glory went to be trained as irregular troops. The most absolute equality prevailed among the Zaporogues while at peace in the marshes of the Don. Then the chiefs, or atamans, when speaking to their subordinates always took their caps off. But during an expedition, on the contrary, their power was unlimited, and disobedience to the captain of the company (Ataman Kotchevoï) was considered the greatest of crimes.

Our filibusters of the seventeenth century have many traits of resemblance to the Zaporogues, and the histories of both preserve the remembrance of prodigies of audacity and of horrible cruelties. Taras Bulba is one of those heroes with whom, as the student of Schiller said, one can only have relations when holding a well-loaded gun in one's hand. I am one of those who have a strong liking for bandits; not because I like to meet them on my road, but because, in spite of myself, the energy these men display in struggling against the whole of society, extorts from me an admiration of which I am ashamed. Formerly I read with delight the lives of Morgan, of Donnais, and of Mombars the destroyer, and I would not be bored if I read them again. However, there are bandits and bandits. Their glory is greatly enhanced if they are of a recent date. Actual bandits always cast into the shade those of the melodrama, and the one who has been more recently hung infallibly effaces the fame of his predecessors. Nowadays neither Mombars nor Taras Bulba can excite so much interest as Mussoni, who last month sustained a regular siege in a wolf's den against five hundred men, who had to attack him by sapping and mining.

Gogol has made brilliantly coloured pictures of his Zaporogues, which please by their very grotesqueness; but sometimes it is too evident that he has not drawn them from nature. Moreover, these character-pictures are framed in such a trivial and romantic setting that one regrets to see them so ill-placed. The most prosaic story would have suited them better than these melodramatic scenes in which are accumulated tragic incidents of famine, torture, etc. In short, one feels that the author is not at ease on the ground which he has chosen; his gait is awkward, and the invariable irony of his style makes the perusal of these melancholy incidents more painful. This style which, in my opinion, is quite out of place in some parts of "Taras Bulba," is much more appropriate in the "Viy," or "King of the Gnomes," a tale of witchcraft, which amuses and alarms at the same time. The grotesque easily blends with the marvellous. Recognising to the full the poetic side of his subject, the author, while describing the savage and strange customs of the old-time Cossacks with his usual precision and exactitude, has easily prepared the way for the introduction of an element of uncanniness.

The receipt for a good, fantastic tale is well known: begin with well-defined portraits of eccentric characters, but such as to be within the bounds of possibility, described with minute realism. From the grotesque to the marvellous the transition is imperceptible, and the reader will find himself in the world of fantasy before he perceives that he has left the real world far behind him. I purposely avoid any attempt to analyse "The King of the Gnomes"; the proper time and place to read it is in the country, by the fireside on a stormy autumn night. After the *dénouement*, it will require a certain amount of resolution to traverse long corridors to reach one's room, while the wind and the rain shake the casements. Now that the fantastic style of the Germans is a little threadbare, that of the Cossacks will have novel charms, and in the first place the merit of resembling nothing else—no slight praise, I think.

The "Memoirs of a Madman" is simultaneously a social satire, a sentimental story, and a medico-legal study of the phenomena presented by a brain which is becoming deranged. The study, I believe, is carefully made and the process carefully depicted, but I do not like this class of writing; madness is one of those misfortunes which arouse pity but which disgust at the same time. Doubtless, by introducing a madman in his story an author is sure of producing an effect. It causes to vibrate a cord which is always susceptible; but it is a cheap method, and Gogol's gifts are such as to be able to dispense with having resort to such. The portrayal of lunatics and dogs—both of whom can produce an irresistible effect—should be left to tyros. It is easy to extract tears from a reader by breaking a poodle's paw. Homer's only excuse, in my opinion, for making us weep at the mutual recognition of the dog Argus and Ulysses, is because he was, I think, the first to discover the resources which the canine race offers to an author at a loss for expedients.

I hasten to go on to a small masterpiece, "An Old-time Household." In a few pages Gogol sketches for us the life of two honest old folk living in the country. There is not a grain of malice in their composition; they are cheated and adored by their servants, and naïve egoists as they are, believe everyone is as happy as themselves. The wife dies. The husband, who only seemed born for merry-making, falls ill and dies some months after his wife. We discover that there was a heart in this mass of flesh. We laugh and weep in turns while reading this charming story, in which the art of the narrator is disguised by simplicity. All is true and natural; every detail is attractive and adds to the general effect.

Translator's Note.—The rest of Merimée's essay is occupied with analyses of Gogol's "Dead Souls" and "The Revisor," and therefore is not given here.

THE MANTLE

In a certain Russian ministerial department——

But it is perhaps better that I do not mention which department it was. There are in the whole of Russia no persons more sensitive than Government officials. Each of them believes if he is annoyed in any way, that the whole official class is insulted in his person.

Recently an Isprawnik (country magistrate)—I do not know of which town—is said to have drawn up a report with the object of showing that, ignoring Government orders, people were speaking of Isprawniks in terms of contempt. In order to prove his assertions, he forwarded with his report a bulky work of fiction, in which on about every tenth page an Isprawnik appeared generally in a drunken condition.

In order therefore to avoid any unpleasantness, I will not definitely indicate the department in which the scene of my story is laid, and will rather say "in a certain chancellery."

Well, in a certain chancellery there was a certain man who, as I cannot deny, was not of an attractive appearance. He was short, had a face marked with smallpox, was rather bald in front, and his forehead and cheeks were deeply lined with furrows—to say nothing of other physical imperfections. Such was the outer aspect of our hero, as produced by the St Petersburg climate.

As regards his official rank—for with us Russians the official rank must always be given—he was what is usually known as a permanent titular councillor, one of those unfortunate beings who, as is well known, are made a butt of by various authors who have the bad habit of attacking people who cannot defend themselves.

Our hero's family name was Bashmatchkin; his baptismal name Akaki Akakievitch. Perhaps the reader may think this name somewhat strange and far-fetched, but he can be assured that it is not so, and that circumstances so arranged it that it was quite impossible to give him any other name.

This happened in the following way. Akaki Akakievitch was born, if I am not mistaken, on the night of the 23rd of March. His deceased mother, the wife of an official and a very good woman, immediately made proper arrangements for his baptism. When the time came, she was lying on the bed before the door. At her right hand stood the godfather, Ivan Ivanovitch Jeroshkin, a very important person, who was registrar of the senate; at her left, the godmother Anna Semenovna Byelobrushkova, the wife of a police inspector, a woman of rare virtues.

Three names were suggested to the mother from which to choose one for the child—Mokuja, Sossuja, or Khozdazat.

"No," she said, "I don't like such names."

14

In order to meet her wishes, the church calendar was opened in another place, and the names Triphiliy, Dula, and Varakhasiy were found.

"This is a punishment from heaven," said the mother. "What sort of names are these! I never heard the like! If it had been Varadat or Varukh, but Triphiliy and Varakhasiy!"

They looked again in the calendar and found Pavsikakhiy and Vakhtisiy.

"Now I see," said the mother, "this is plainly fate. If there is no help for it, then he had better take his father's name, which was Akaki."

So the child was called Akaki Akakievitch. It was baptised, although it wept and cried and made all kinds of grimaces, as though it had a presentiment that it would one day be a titular councillor.

We have related all this so conscientiously that the reader himself might be convinced that it was impossible for the little Akaki to receive any other name. When and how he entered the chancellery and who appointed him, no one could remember. However many of his superiors might come and go, he was always seen in the same spot, in the same attitude, busy with the same work, and bearing the same title; so that people began to believe he had come into the world just as he was, with his bald forehead and official uniform.

In the chancellery where he worked, no kind of notice was taken of him. Even the office attendants did not rise from their seats when he entered, nor look at him; they took no more notice than if a fly had flown through the room. His superiors treated him in a coldly despotic manner. The assistant of the head of the department, when he pushed a pile of papers under his nose, did not even say "Please copy those," or "There is something interesting for you," or make any other polite remark such as well-educated officials are in the habit of doing. But Akaki took the documents, without worrying himself whether they had the right to hand them over to him or not, and straightway set to work to copy them.

His young colleagues made him the butt of their ridicule and their elegant wit, so far as officials can be said to possess any wit. They did not scruple to relate in his presence various tales of their own invention regarding his manner of life and his landlady, who was seventy years old. They declared that she beat him, and inquired of him when he would lead her to the marriage altar. Sometimes they let a shower of scraps of paper fall on his head, and told him they were snowflakes.

But Akaki Akakievitch made no answer to all these attacks; he seemed oblivious of their presence. His work was not affected in the slightest degree; during all these interruptions he did not make a single error in copying.

16

Only when the horse-play grew intolerable, when he was held by the arm and prevented writing, he would say "Do leave me alone! Why do you always want to disturb me at work?" There was something peculiarly pathetic in these words and the way in which he uttered them.

One day it happened that when a young clerk, who had been recently appointed to the chancellery, prompted by the example of the others, was playing him some trick, he suddenly seemed arrested by something in the tone of Akaki's voice, and from that moment regarded the old official with quite different eyes. He felt as though some supernatural power drew him away from the colleagues whose acquaintance he had made here, and whom he had hitherto regarded as well-educated, respectable men, and alienated him from them. Long afterwards, when surrounded by gay companions, he would see the figure of the poor little councillor and hear the words "Do leave me alone! Why will you always disturb me at work?" Along with these words, he also heard others: "Am I not your brother?" On such occasions the young man would hide his face in his hands, and think how little humane feeling after all was to be found in men's hearts; how much coarseness and cruelty was to be found even in the educated and those who were everywhere regarded as good and honourable men.

Never was there an official who did his work so zealously as Akaki Akakievitch. "Zealously," do I say? He worked with a passionate love of his task. While he copied official documents, a world of varied beauty rose before his eyes. His delight in copying was legible in his face. To form certain letters afforded him special satisfaction, and when he came to them he was quite another man; he began to smile, his eyes sparkled, and he pursed up his lips, so that those who knew him could see by his face which letters he was working at.

Had he been rewarded according to his zeal, he would perhaps—to his own astonishment—have been raised to the rank of civic councillor. However, he was not destined, as his colleagues expressed it, to wear a cross at his buttonhole, but only to get hæmorrhoids by leading a too sedentary life.

For the rest, I must mention that on one occasion he attracted a certain amount of attention. A director, who was a kindly man and wished to reward him for his long service, ordered that he should be entrusted with a task more important than the documents which he usually had to copy. This consisted in preparing a report for a court, altering the headings of various documents, and here and there changing the first personal pronoun into the third.

Akaki undertook the work; but it confused and exhausted him to such a degree that the sweat ran from his forehead and he at last exclaimed: "No! Please give me again something to copy." From that time he was allowed to continue copying to his life's end.

Outside this copying nothing appeared to exist for him. He did not even think of his clothes. His uniform, which was originally green, had acquired a reddish tint. The collar was so narrow and so tight that his neck, although of average length, stretched far out of it, and appeared extraordinarily long, just like those of the cats with movable heads, which are carried about on trays and sold to the peasants in Russian villages.

Something was always sticking to his clothes—a piece of thread, a fragment of straw which had been flying about, etc. Moreover he seemed to have a special predilection for passing under windows just when something not very clean was being thrown out of them, and therefore he constantly carried about on his hat pieces of orange-peel and such refuse. He never took any notice of what was going on in the streets, in contrast to his colleagues who were always watching people closely and whom nothing delighted more than to see someone walking along on the opposite pavement with a rent in his trousers.

But Akaki Akakievitch saw nothing but the clean, regular lines of his copies before him; and only when he collided suddenly with a horse's nose, which blew its breath noisily in his face, did the good man observe that he was not sitting at his writing-table among his neat duplicates, but walking in the middle of the street.

When he arrived home, he sat down at once to supper, ate his cabbage-soup hurriedly, and then, without taking any notice how it tasted, a slice of beef with garlic, together with the flies and any other trifles which happened to be lying on it. As soon as his hunger was satisfied, he set himself to write, and began to copy the documents which he had brought home with him. If he happened to have no official documents to copy, he copied for his own satisfaction political letters, not for their more or less grand style but because they were directed to some high personage.

When the grey St Petersburg sky is darkened by the veil of night, and the whole of officialdom has finished its dinner according to its gastronomical inclinations or the depth of its purse—when all recover themselves from the perpetual scratching of bureaucratic pens, and all the cares and business with which men so often needlessly burden themselves, they devote the evening to recreation. One goes to the theatre; another roams about the streets, inspecting toilettes; another whispers flattering words to some young girl who has risen like a star in his modest official circle. Here and there one visits a colleague in his third or fourth story flat, consisting of two rooms with an entrance-hall and kitchen, fitted with some pretentious articles of furniture purchased by many abstinences.

In short, at this time every official betakes himself to some form of recreation—playing whist, drinking tea, and eating cheap pastry or smoking tobacco in long pipes. Some relate scandals about great people, for in whatever situation of life the Russian may be, he always likes to hear about the aristocracy; others recount well-worn but popular anecdotes, as for example that of the commandant to whom it was reported that a rogue had cut off the horse's tail on the monument of Peter the Great.

But even at this time of rest and recreation, Akaki Akakievitch remained faithful to his habits. No one could say that he had ever seen him in any evening social circle. After he had written as much as he wanted, he went to bed, and thought of the joys of the coming day, and the fine copies which God would give him to do.

So flowed on the peaceful existence of a man who was quite content with his post and his income of four hundred roubles a year. He might perhaps have reached an extreme old age if one of those unfortunate events had not befallen him, which not only happen to titular but to actual privy, court, and other councillors, and also to persons who never give advice nor receive it.

In St Petersburg all those who draw a salary of four hundred roubles or thereabouts have a terrible enemy in our northern cold, although some assert that it is very good for the health. About nine o'clock in the morning, when the clerks of the various departments betake themselves to their offices, the cold nips their noses so vigorously that most of them are quite bewildered. If at this time even high officials so suffer from the severity of the cold in their own persons that the tears come into their eyes, what must be the sufferings of the titular councillors, whose means do not allow of their protecting themselves against the rigour of winter? When they have put on their light cloaks, they must hurry through five or six streets as rapidly as possible, and then in the porter's lodge warm themselves and wait till their frozen official faculties have thawed.

For some time Akaki had been feeling on his back and shoulders very sharp twinges of pain, although he ran as fast as possible from his dwelling to the office. After well considering the matter, he came to the conclusion that these were due to the imperfections of his cloak. In his room he examined it carefully, and discovered that in two or three places it had become so thin as to be quite transparent, and that the lining was much torn.

This cloak had been for a long time the standing object of jests on the part of Akaki's merciless colleagues. They had even robbed it of the noble name of "cloak," and called it a cowl. It certainly presented a remarkable appearance. Every year the collar had grown smaller, for every year the poor titular councillor had taken a piece of it away in order to repair some other part of the cloak; and these repairs did not look as if they had been done by the skilled hand of a tailor.

They had been executed in a very clumsy way and looked remarkably ugly.

After Akaki Akakievitch had ended his melancholy examination, he said to himself that he must certainly take his cloak to Petrovitch the tailor, who lived high up in a dark den on the fourth floor.

With his squinting eyes and pock-marked face, Petrovitch certainly did not look as if he had the honour to make frock-coats and trousers for high officials—that is to say, when he was sober, and not absorbed in more pleasant diversions.

I might dispense here with dwelling on this tailor; but since it is the custom to portray the physiognomy of every separate personage in a tale, I must give a better or worse description of Petrovitch. Formerly when he was a simple serf in his master's house, he was merely called Gregor. When he became free, he thought he ought to adorn himself with a new name, and dubbed himself Petrovitch; at the same time he began to drink lustily, not only on the high festivals but on all those which are marked with a cross in the calendar. By thus solemnly celebrating the days consecrated by the Church, he considered that he was remaining faithful to the traditions of his childhood; and when he quarrelled with his wife, he shouted that she was an earthly minded creature and a German. Of this lady we have nothing more to relate than that she was the wife of Petrovitch, and that she did not wear a kerchief but a cap on her head. For the rest, she was not pretty; only the soldiers looked at her as they passed, then they twirled their moustaches and walked on, laughing.

Akaki Akakievitch accordingly betook himself to the tailor's attic. He reached it by a dark, dirty, damp staircase, from which, as in all the inhabited houses of the poorer class in St Petersburg, exhaled an effluvia of spirits vexatious to nose and eyes alike. As the titular councillor climbed these slippery stairs, he calculated what sum Petrovitch could reasonably ask for repairing his cloak, and determined only to give him a rouble.

The door of the tailor's flat stood open in order to provide an outlet for the clouds of smoke which rolled from the kitchen, where Petrovitch's wife was just then cooking fish. Akaki, his eyes smarting, passed through the kitchen without her seeing him, and entered the room where the tailor sat on a large, roughly made, wooden table, his legs crossed like those of a Turkish pasha, and, as is the custom of tailors, with bare feet. What first arrested attention, when one approached him, was his thumb nail, which was a little misshapen but as hard and strong as the shell of a tortoise. Round his neck were hung several skeins of thread, and on his knees lay a tattered coat. For some minutes he had been trying in vain to thread his needle. He was first of all angry with the gathering darkness, then with the thread.

"Why the deuce won't you go in, you worthless scoundrel!" he exclaimed.

Akaki saw at once that he had come at an inopportune moment. He wished he had found Petrovitch at a more favourable time, when he was enjoying himself—when, as his wife expressed it, he was having a substantial ration of brandy. At such times the tailor was extraordinarily ready to meet his customer's proposals with bows and gratitude to boot. Sometimes indeed his wife interfered in the transaction, and declared that he was drunk and promised to do the work at much too low a price; but if the customer paid a trifle more, the matter was settled.

Unfortunately for the titular councillor, Petrovitch had just now not yet touched the brandy flask. At such moments he was hard, obstinate, and ready to demand an exorbitant price.

Akaki foresaw this danger, and would gladly have turned back again, but it was already too late. The tailor's single eye—for he was one-eyed—had already noticed him, and Akaki Akakievitch murmured involuntarily "Good day, Petrovitch."

"Welcome, sir," answered the tailor, and fastened his glance on the titular councillor's hand to see what he had in it.

"I come just—merely—in order—I want—"

We must here remark that the modest titular councillor was in the habit of expressing his thoughts only by prepositions, adverbs, or particles, which never yielded a distinct meaning. If the matter of which he spoke was a difficult one, he could never finish the sentence he had begun. So that when transacting business, he generally entangled himself in the formula "Yes—it is indeed true that——" Then he would remain standing and forget what he wished to say, or believe that he had said it.

"What do you want, sir?" asked Petrovitch, scrutinising him from top to toe with a searching look, and contemplating his collar, sleeves, coat, buttons—in short his whole uniform, although he knew them all very well, having made them himself. That is the way of tailors whenever they meet an acquaintance.

Then Akaki answered, stammering as usual, "I want—Petrovitch—this cloak—you see—it is still quite good, only a little dusty—and therefore it looks a little old. It is, however, still quite new, only that it is worn a little—there in the back and here in the shoulder—and there are three quite little splits. You see it is hardly worth talking about; it can be thoroughly repaired in a few minutes."

Petrovitch took the unfortunate cloak, spread it on the table, contemplated it in silence, and shook his head. Then he stretched his hand towards the window-sill for his snuff-box, a round one with the portrait of a general on the lid. I do not know whose portrait it was, for it had been accidentally injured, and the ingenious tailor had gummed a piece of paper over it.

After Petrovitch had taken a pinch of snuff, he examined the cloak again, held it to the light, and once more shook his head. Then he examined the lining, took a second pinch of snuff, and at last exclaimed, "No! that is a wretched rag! It is beyond repair!"

At these words Akaki's courage fell.

"What!" he cried in the querulous tone of a child. "Can this hole really not be repaired? Look! Petrovitch; there are only two rents, and you have enough pieces of cloth to mend them with."

"Yes, I have enough pieces of cloth; but how should I sew them on? The stuff is quite worn out; it won't bear another stitch."

"Well, can't you strengthen it with another piece of cloth?"

"No, it won't bear anything more; cloth after all is only cloth, and in its present condition a gust of wind might blow the wretched mantle into tatters."

"But if you could only make it last a little longer, do you see—really——"

"No!" answered Petrovitch decidedly. "There is nothing more to be done with it; it is completely worn out. It would be better if you made yourself foot bandages out of it for the winter; they are warmer than stockings. It was the Germans who invented stockings for their own profit." Petrovitch never lost an opportunity of having a hit at the Germans. "You must certainly buy a new cloak," he added.

"A new cloak?" exclaimed Akaki Akakievitch, and it grew dark before his eyes. The tailor's work-room seemed to go round with him, and the only object he could clearly distinguish was the paper-patched general's portrait on the tailor's snuff-box. "A new cloak!" he murmured, as though half asleep. "But I have no money."

"Yes, a new cloak," repeated Petrovitch with cruel calmness.

"Well, even if I did decide on it—how much——"

"You mean how much would it cost?"

"Yes."

"About a hundred and fifty roubles," answered the tailor, pursing his lips. This diabolical tailor took a special pleasure in embarrassing his customers and watching the expression of their faces with his squinting single eye.

"A hundred and fifty roubles for a cloak!" exclaimed Akaki Akakievitch in a tone which sounded like an outcry—possibly the first he had uttered since his birth.

"Yes," replied Petrovitch. "And then the marten-fur collar and silk lining for the hood would make it up to two hundred roubles."

28

"Petrovitch, I adjure you!" said Akaki Akakievitch in an imploring tone, no longer hearing nor wishing to hear the tailor's words, "try to make this cloak last me a little longer."

"No, it would be a useless waste of time and work."

After this answer, Akaki departed, feeling quite crushed; while Petrovitch, with his lips firmly pursed up, feeling pleased with himself for his firmness and brave defence of the art of tailoring, remained sitting on the table.

Meanwhile Akaki wandered about the streets like a somnambulist, at random and without an object. "What a terrible business!" he said to himself. "Really, I could never have believed that it would come to that. No," he continued after a short pause, "I could not have guessed that it would come to that. Now I find myself in a completely unexpected situation—in a difficulty that——"

As he thus continued his monologue, instead of approaching his dwelling, he went, without noticing it, in quite a wrong direction. A chimney-sweep brushed against him and blackened his back as he passed by. From a house where building was going on, a bucket of plaster of Paris was emptied on his head. But he saw and heard nothing. Only when he collided with a sentry, who, after he had planted his halberd beside him, was shaking out some snuff from his snuff-box with a bony hand, was he startled out of his reverie.

"What do you want?" the rough guardian of civic order exclaimed. "Can't you walk on the pavement properly?"

This sudden address at last completely roused Akaki from his torpid condition. He collected his thoughts, considered his situation clearly, and began to take counsel with himself seriously and frankly, as with a friend to whom one entrusts the most intimate secrets.

"No!" he said at last. "To-day I will get nothing from Petrovitch—to-day he is in a bad humour—perhaps his wife has beaten him—I will look him up again next Sunday. On Saturday evenings he gets intoxicated; then the next day he wants a pick-me-up—his wife gives him no money—I squeeze a ten-kopeck piece into his hand; then he will be more reasonable and we can discuss the cloak further."

Encouraged by these reflections, Akaki waited patiently till Sunday. On that day, having seen Petrovitch's wife leave the house, he betook himself to the tailor's and found him, as he had expected, in a very depressed state as the result of his Saturday's dissipation. But hardly had Akaki let a word fall about the mantle than the diabolical tailor awoke from his torpor and exclaimed, "No, nothing can be done; you must certainly buy a new cloak."

The titular councillor pressed a ten-kopeck piece into his hand.

"Thanks, my dear friend," said Petrovitch; "that will get me a pick-me-up, and I will drink your health with it. But as for your old mantle, what is the use of talking about it? It isn't worth a farthing. Let me only get to work; I will make you a splendid one, I promise!"

But poor Akaki Akakievitch still importuned the tailor to repair his old one.

"No, and again no," answered Petrovitch. "It is quite impossible. Trust me; I won't take you in. I will even put silver hooks and eyes on the collar, as is now the fashion."

This time Akaki saw that he must follow the tailor's advice, and again all his courage sank. He must have a new mantle made. But how should he pay for it? He certainly expected a Christmas bonus at the office; but that money had been allotted beforehand. He must buy a pair of trousers, and pay his shoemaker for repairing two pairs of boots, and buy some fresh linen. Even if, by an unexpected stroke of good luck, the director raised the usual bonus from forty to fifty roubles, what was such a small amount in comparison with the immense sum which Petrovitch demanded? A mere drop of water in the sea.

At any rate, he might expect that Petrovitch, if he were in a good humour, would lower the price of the cloak to eighty roubles; but where were these eighty roubles to be found? Perhaps he might succeed if he left no stone unturned, in raising half the sum; but he saw no means of procuring the other half. As regards the first half, he had been in the habit, as often as he received a rouble, of placing a kopeck in a money-box. At the end of each half-year he changed these copper coins for silver. He had been doing this for some time, and his savings just now amounted to forty roubles. Thus he already had half the required sum. But the other half!

Akaki made long calculations, and at last determined that he must, at least for a whole year, reduce some of his daily expenses. He would have to give up his tea in the evening, and copy his documents in his landlady's room, in order to economise the fuel in his own. He also resolved to avoid rough pavements as much as possible, in order to spare his shoes; and finally to give out less washing to the laundress.

At first he found these deprivations rather trying; but gradually he got accustomed to them, and at last took to going to bed without any supper at all. Although his body suffered from this abstinence, his spirit derived all the richer nutriment from perpetually thinking about his new cloak. From that time it seemed as though his nature had completed itself; as though he had married and possessed a companion on his life journey. This companion was the thought of his new cloak, properly wadded and lined.

From that time he became more lively, and his character grew stronger, like that of a man who has set a goal before himself which he will reach at all costs. All that was indecisive and vague in his gait and gestures had disappeared. A new fire began to gleam in his eyes, and in his bold dreams he sometimes even proposed to himself the question whether he should not have a marten-fur collar made for his coat.

These and similar thoughts sometimes caused him to be absent-minded. As he was copying his documents one day he suddenly noticed that he had made a slip. "Ugh!" he exclaimed, and crossed himself.

At least once a month he went to Petrovitch to discuss the precious cloak with him, and to settle many important questions, e.g. where and at what price he should buy the cloth, and what colour he should choose.

Each of these visits gave rise to new discussions, but he always returned home in a happier mood, feeling that at last the day must come when all the materials would have been bought and the cloak would be lying ready to put on.

This great event happened sooner than he had hoped. The director gave him a bonus, not of forty or fifty, but of five-and-sixty roubles. Had the worthy official noticed that Akaki needed a new mantle, or was the exceptional amount of the gift only due to chance?

However that might be, Akaki was now richer by twenty roubles. Such an access of wealth necessarily hastened his important undertaking. After two or three more months of enduring hunger, he had collected his eighty roubles. His heart, generally so quiet, began to beat violently; he hastened to Petrovitch, who accompanied him to a draper's shop. There, without hesitating, they bought a very fine piece of cloth. For more than half a year they had discussed the matter incessantly, and gone round the shops inquiring prices. Petrovitch examined the cloth, and said they would not find anything better. For the lining they chose a piece of such firm and thickly woven linen that the tailor declared it was better than silk; it also had a splendid gloss on it. They did not buy marten fur, for it was too dear, but chose the best catskin in the shop, which was a very good imitation of the former.

It took Petrovitch quite fourteen days to make the mantle, for he put an extra number of stitches into it. He charged twelve roubles for his work, and said he could not ask less; it was all sewn with silk, and the tailor smoothed the sutures with his teeth.

At last the day came—I cannot name it certainly, but it assuredly was the most solemn in Akaki's life—when the tailor brought the cloak. He brought it early in the morning, before the titular councillor started for his office. He could not have come at a more suitable moment, for the cold had again begun to be very severe.

Petrovitch entered the room with the dignified mien of an important tailor. His face wore a peculiarly serious expression, such as Akaki had never seen on it. He was fully conscious of his dignity, and of the gulf which separates the tailor who only repairs old clothes from the artist who makes new ones.

The cloak had been brought wrapped up in a large, new, freshly washed handkerchief, which the tailor carefully opened, folded, and placed in his pocket. Then he proudly took the cloak in both hands and laid it on Akaki Akakievitch's shoulders. He pulled it straight behind to see how it hung majestically in its whole length. Finally he wished to see the effect it made when unbuttoned. Akaki, however, wished to try the sleeves, which fitted wonderfully well. In brief, the cloak was irreproachable, and its fit and cut left nothing to be desired.

While the tailor was contemplating his work, he did not forget to say that the only reason he had charged so little for making it, was that he had only a low rent to pay and had known Akaki Akakievitch for a long time; he declared that any tailor who lived on the Nevski Prospect would have charged at least five-and-sixty roubles for making up such a cloak.

The titular councillor did not let himself be involved in a discussion on the subject. He thanked him, paid him, and then sallied forth on his way to the office.

Petrovitch went out with him, and remained standing in the street to watch Akaki as long as possible wearing the mantle; then he hurried through a cross-alley and came into the main street again to catch another glimpse of him.

Akaki went on his way in high spirits. Every moment he was acutely conscious of having a new cloak on, and smiled with sheer self-complacency. His head was filled with only two ideas: first that the cloak was warm, and secondly that it was beautiful. Without noticing anything on the road, he marched straight to the chancellery, took off his treasure in the hall, and solemnly entrusted it to the porter's care.

I do not know how the report spread in the office that Akaki's old cloak had ceased to exist. All his colleagues hastened to see his splendid new one, and then began to congratulate him so warmly that he at first had to smile with self-satisfaction, but finally began to feel embarrassed.

But how great was his surprise when his cruel colleagues remarked that he should formally "handsel" his cloak by giving them a feast! Poor Akaki was so disconcerted and taken aback, that he did not know what to answer nor how to excuse himself. He stammered out, blushing, that the cloak was not so new as it appeared; it was really second-hand.

One of his superiors, who probably wished to show that he was not too proud of his rank and title, and did not disdain social intercourse with his subordinates, broke in and said, "Gentlemen! Instead of Akaki Akakievitch, I will invite you to a little meal. Come to tea with me this evening. To-day happens to be my birthday."

All the others thanked him for his kind proposal, and joyfully accepted his invitation. Akaki at first wished to decline, but was told that to do so would be grossly impolite and unpardonable, so he reconciled himself to the inevitable. Moreover, he felt a certain satisfaction at the thought that the occasion would give him a new opportunity of displaying his cloak in the streets. This whole day for him was like a festival day. In the cheerfullest possible mood he returned home, took off his cloak, and hung it up on the wall after once more examining the cloth and the lining. Then he took out his old one in order to compare it with Petrovitch's masterpiece. His looks passed from one to the other, and he thought to himself, smiling, "What a difference!"

He ate his supper cheerfully, and after he had finished, did not sit down as usual to copy documents. No; he lay down, like a Sybarite, on the sofa and waited. When the time came, he made his toilette, took his cloak, and went out.

I cannot say where was the house of the superior official who so graciously invited his subordinates to tea. My memory begins to grow weak, and the innumerable streets and houses of St Petersburg go round so confusedly in my head that I have difficulty in finding my way about them. So much, however, is certain: that the honourable official lived in a very fine quarter of the city, and therefore very far from Akaki Akakievitch's dwelling.

At first the titular councillor traversed several badly lit streets which seemed quite empty; but the nearer he approached his superior's house, the more brilliant and lively the streets became. He met many people, among whom were elegantly dressed ladies, and men with beaverskin collars. The peasants' sledges, with their wooden seats and brass studs, became rarer; while now every moment appeared skilled coachmen with velvet caps, driving lacquered sleighs covered with bearskins, and fine carriages.

At last he reached the house whither he had been invited. His host lived in a first-rate style; a lamp hung before his door, and he occupied the whole of the second story. As Akaki entered the vestibule, he saw a long row of galoshes; on a table a samovar was smoking and hissing; many cloaks, some of them adorned with velvet and fur collars, hung on the wall. In the adjoining room he heard a confused noise, which assumed a more decided character when a servant opened the door and came out bearing a tray full of empty cups, a milk-jug, and a basket of biscuits. Evidently the guests had been there some time and had already drunk their first cup of tea.

After hanging his cloak on a peg, Akaki approached the room in which his colleagues, smoking long pipes, were sitting round the card-table and making a good deal of noise. He entered the room, but remained standing by the door, not knowing what to do; but his colleagues greeted him with loud applause, and all hastened into the vestibule to take another look at his cloak. This excitement quite robbed the good titular councillor of his composure; but in his simplicity of heart he rejoiced at the praises which were lavished on his precious cloak. Soon afterwards his colleagues left him to himself and resumed their whist parties.

Akaki felt much embarrassed, and did not know what to do with his feet and hands. Finally he sat down by the players; looked now at their faces and now at the cards; then he yawned and remembered that it was long past his usual bedtime. He made an attempt to go, but they held him back and told him that he could not do so without drinking a glass of champagne on what was for him such a memorable day.

Soon supper was brought. It consisted of cold veal, cakes, and pastry of various kinds, accompanied by several bottles of champagne. Akaki was obliged to drink two glasses of it, and found everything round him take on a more cheerful aspect. But he could not forget that it was already midnight and that he ought to have been in bed long ago. From fear of being kept back again, he slipped furtively into the vestibule, where he was pained to find his cloak lying on the ground. He carefully shook it, brushed it, put it on, and went out.

The street-lamps were still alight. Some of the small ale-houses frequented by servants and the lower classes were still open, and some had just been shut; but by the beams of light which shone through the chinks of the doors, it was easy to see that there were still people inside, probably male and female domestics, who were quite indifferent to their employers' interests.

Akaki Akakievitch turned homewards in a cheerful mood. Suddenly he found himself in a long street where it was very quiet by day and still more so at night. The surroundings were very dismal. Only here and there hung a lamp which threatened to go out for want of oil; there were long rows of wooden houses with wooden fences, but no sign of a living soul. Only the snow in the street glimmered faintly in the dim light of the half-extinguished lanterns, and the little houses looked melancholy in the darkness.

Akaki went on till the street opened into an enormous square, on the other side of which the houses were scarcely visible, and which looked like a terrible desert. At a great distance—God knows where!—glimmered the light in a sentry-box, which seemed to stand at the end of the world. At the same moment Akaki's cheerful mood vanished. He went in the direction of the light with a vague sense of depression, as though some mischief threatened him. On the way he kept looking round him with alarm. The huge, melancholy expanse looked to him like a sea. "No," he thought to himself, "I had better not look at it"; and he continued his way with his eyes fixed on the ground. When he raised them again he suddenly saw just in front of him several men with long moustaches, whose faces he could not distinguish. Everything grew dark before his eyes, and his heart seemed to be constricted.

"That is my cloak!" shouted one of the men, and seized him by the collar. Akaki tried to call for help. Another man pressed a great bony fist on his mouth, and said to him, "Just try to scream again!" At the same moment the unhappy titular councillor felt the cloak snatched away from him, and simultaneously received a kick which stretched him senseless in the snow. A few minutes later he came to himself and stood up; but there was no longer anyone in sight. Robbed of his cloak, and feeling frozen to the marrow, he began to shout with all his might; but his voice did not reach the end of the huge square. Continuing to shout, he ran with the rage of despair to the sentinel in the sentry-box, who, leaning on his halberd, asked him why the deuce he was making such a hellish noise and running so violently.

When Akaki reached the sentinel, he accused him of being drunk because he did not see that passers-by were robbed a short distance from his sentry-box.

"I saw you quite well," answered the sentinel, "in the middle of the square with two men; I thought you were friends. It is no good getting so excited. Go to-morrow to the police inspector; he will take up the matter, have the thieves searched for, and make an examination."

Akaki saw there was nothing to be done but to go home. He reached his dwelling in a state of dreadful disorder, his hair hanging wildly over his forehead, and his clothes covered with snow. When his old landlady heard him knocking violently at the door, she sprang up and hastened thither, only half-dressed; but at the sight of Akaki started back in alarm. When he told her what had happened, she clasped her hands together and said, "You should not go to the police inspector, but to the municipal Superintendent of the district. The inspector will put you off with fine words, and do nothing; but I have known the Superintendent for a long time. My former cook, Anna, is now in his service, and I often see him pass by under our windows. He goes to church on all the festival-days, and one sees at once by his looks that he is an honest man."

After hearing this eloquent recommendation, Akaki retired sadly to his room. Those who can picture to themselves such a situation will understand what sort of a night he passed. As early as possible the next morning he went to the Superintendent's house. The servants told him that he was still asleep. At ten o'clock he returned, only to receive the same reply. At twelve o'clock the Superintendent had gone out.

About dinner-time the titular councillor called again, but the clerks asked him in a severe tone what was his business with their superior. Then for the first time in his life Akaki displayed an energetic character. He declared that it was absolutely necessary for him to speak with the Superintendent on an official matter, and that anyone who ventured to put difficulties in his way would have to pay dearly for it.

This left them without reply. One of the clerks departed, in order to deliver his message. When Akaki was admitted to the Superintendent's presence, the latter's way of receiving his story was somewhat singular. Instead of confining himself to the principal matter—the theft, he asked the titular councillor how he came to be out so late, and whether he had not been in suspicious company.

Taken aback by such a question, Akaki did not know what to answer, and went away without knowing whether any steps would be taken in the matter or not.

The whole day he had not been in his office—a perfectly new event in his life. The next day he appeared there again with a pale face and restless aspect, in his old cloak, which looked more wretched than ever. When his colleagues heard of his misfortune, some were cruel enough to laugh; most of them, however, felt a sincere sympathy with him, and started a subscription for his benefit; but this praiseworthy undertaking had only a very insignificant result, because these same officials had been lately called upon to contribute to two other subscriptions—in the first case to purchase a portrait of their director, and in the second to buy a work which a friend of his had published.

One of them, who felt sincerely sorry for Akaki, gave him some good advice for want of something better. He told him it was a waste of time to go again to the Superintendent, because even in case that this official succeeded in recovering the cloak, the police would keep it till the titular councillor had indisputably proved that he was the real owner of it. Akaki's friend suggested to him to go to a certain important personage, who because of his connection with the authorities could expedite the matter.

In his bewilderment, Akaki resolved to follow this advice. It was not known what position this personage occupied, nor how high it really was; the only facts known were that he had only recently been placed in it, and that there must be still higher personages than himself, as he was leaving no stone unturned in order to get promotion. When he entered his private room, he made his subordinates wait for him on the stairs below, and no one had direct access to him. If anyone called with a request to see him, the secretary of the board informed the Government secretary, who in his turn passed it on to a higher official, and the latter informed the important personage himself.

That is the way business is carried on in our Holy Russia. In the endeavour to resemble the higher officials, everyone imitates the manners of his superiors. Not long ago a titular councillor, who was appointed to the headship of a little office, immediately placed over the door of one of his two tiny rooms the inscription "Council-chamber." Outside it were placed servants with red collars and lace-work on their coats, in order to announce petitioners, and to conduct them into the chamber which was hardly large enough to contain a chair.

But let us return to the important personage in question. His way of carrying things on was dignified and imposing, but a trifle complicated. His system might be summed up in a single word—"severity." This word he would repeat in a sonorous tone three times in succession, and the last time turn a piercing look on the person with whom he happened to be speaking. He might have spared himself the trouble of displaying so much disciplinary energy; the ten officials who were under his command feared him quite sufficiently without it. As soon as they were aware of his approach, they would lay down their pens, and hasten to station themselves in a respectful attitude as he passed by. In converse with his subordinates, he preserved a stiff, unbending attitude, and generally confined himself to such expressions as "What do you want? Do you know with whom you are speaking? Do you consider who is in front of you?"

For the rest, he was a good-natured man, friendly and amiable with his acquaintances. But the title of "District-Superintendent" had turned his head. Since the time when it had been bestowed upon him, he lived for a great part of the day in a kind of dizzy self-intoxication. Among his equals, however, he recovered his equilibrium, and then showed his real amiability in more than one direction; but as soon as he found himself in the society of anyone of less rank than himself, he entrenched himself in a severe taciturnity. This situation was all the more painful for him as he was quite aware that he might have passed his time more agreeably.

All who watched him at such moments perceived clearly that he longed to take part in an interesting conversation, but that the fear of displaying some unguarded courtesy, of appearing too confidential, and thereby doing a deadly injury to his dignity, held him back. In order to avoid such a risk, he maintained an unnatural reserve, and only spoke from time to time in monosyllables. He had driven this habit to such a pitch that people called him "The Tedious," and the title was well deserved.

Such was the person to whose aid Akaki wished to appeal. The moment at which he came seemed expressly calculated to flatter the Superintendent's vanity, and accordingly to help forward the titular councillor's cause.

The high personage was seated in his office, talking cheerfully with an old friend whom he had not seen for several years, when he was told that a gentleman named Akakievitch begged for the honour of an interview.

"Who is the man?" asked the Superintendent in a contemptuous tone.

"An official," answered the servant.

"He must wait. I have no time to receive him now."

The high personage lied; there was nothing in the way of his granting the desired audience. His friend and himself had already quite exhausted various topics of conversation. Many long, embarrassing pauses had occurred, during which they had lightly tapped each other on the shoulder, saying, "So it was, you see."

"Yes, Stepan."

But the Superintendent refused to receive the petitioner, in order to show his friend, who had quitted the public service and lived in the country, his own importance, and how officials must wait in the vestibule till he chose to receive them.

At last, after they had discussed various other subjects with other intervals of silence, during which the two friends leaned back in their chairs and blew cigarette smoke in the air, the Superintendent seemed suddenly to remember that someone had sought an interview with him. He called the secretary, who stood with a roll of papers in his hand at the door, and told him to admit the petitioner.

When he saw Akaki approaching with his humble expression, wearing his shabby old uniform, he turned round suddenly towards him and said "What do you want?" in a severe voice, accompanied by a vibrating intonation which at the time of receiving his promotion he had practised before the looking-glass for eight days.

The modest Akaki was quite taken aback by his harsh manner; however, he made an effort to recover his composure, and to relate how his cloak had been stolen, but did not do so without encumbering his narrative with a mass of superfluous detail. He added that he had applied to His Excellence in the hope that through his making a representation to the police inspector, or some other high personage, the cloak might be traced.

The Superintendent found Akaki's method of procedure somewhat unofficial. "Ah, sir," he said, "don't you know what steps you ought to take in such a case? Don't you know the proper procedure? You should have handed in your petition at the chancellery. This in due course would have passed through the hands of the chief clerk and director of the bureau. It would then have been brought before my secretary, who would have made a communication to you."

"Allow me," replied Akaki, making a strenuous effort to preserve the remnants of his presence of mind, for he felt that the perspiration stood on his forehead, "allow me to remark to Your Excellence that I ventured to trouble you personally in this matter because secretaries—secretaries are a hopeless kind of people."

"What! How! Is it possible?" exclaimed the Superintendent. "How could you say such a thing? Where have you got your ideas from? It is disgraceful to see young people so rebellious towards their superiors." In his official zeal the Superintendent overlooked the fact that the titular councillor was well on in the fifties, and that the word "young" could only apply to him conditionally, i.e. in comparison with a man of seventy. "Do you also know," he continued, "with whom you are speaking? Do you consider before whom you are standing? Do you consider, I ask you, do you consider?" As he spoke, he stamped his foot, and his voice grew deeper.

Akaki was quite upset—nay, thoroughly frightened; he trembled and shook and could hardly remain standing upright. Unless one of the office servants had hurried to help him, he would have fallen to the ground. As it was, he was dragged out almost unconscious.

But the Superintendent was quite delighted at the effect he had produced. It exceeded all his expectations, and filled with satisfaction at the fact that his words made such an impression on a middle-aged man that he lost consciousness, he cast a side-glance at his friend to see what effect the scene had produced on him. His self-satisfaction was further increased when he observed that his friend also was moved, and looked at him half-timidly.

Akaki had no idea how he got down the stairs and crossed the street, for he felt more dead than alive. In his whole life he had never been so scolded by a superior official, let alone one whom he had never seen before.

He wandered in the storm which raged without taking the least care of himself, nor sheltering himself on the sidewalk against its fury. The wind, which blew from all sides and out of all the narrow streets, caused him to contract inflammation of the throat. When he reached home he was unable to speak a word, and went straight to bed.

Such was the result of the Superintendent's lecture.

The next day Akaki had a violent fever. Thanks to the St Petersburg climate, his illness developed with terrible rapidity. When the doctor came, he saw that the case was already hopeless; he felt his pulse and ordered him some poultices, merely in order that he should not die without some medical help, and declared at once that he had only two days to live. After giving this opinion, he said to Akaki's landlady, "There is no time to be lost; order a pine coffin, for an oak one would be too expensive for this poor man."

Whether the titular councillor heard these words, whether they excited him and made him lament his tragic lot, no one ever knew, for he was delirious all the time. Strange pictures passed incessantly through his weakened brain. At one time he saw Petrovitch the tailor and asked him to make a cloak with nooses attached for the thieves who persecuted him in bed, and begged his old landlady to chase away the robbers who were hidden under his coverlet. At another time he seemed to be listening to the Superintendent's severe reprimand, and asking his forgiveness. Then he uttered such strange and confused remarks that the old woman crossed herself in alarm. She had never heard anything of the kind in her life, and these ravings astonished her all the more because the expression "Your Excellency" constantly occurred in them. Later on he murmured wild disconnected words, from which it could only be gathered that his thoughts were continually revolving round a cloak.

At last Akaki breathed his last. Neither his room nor his cupboard were officially sealed up, for the simple reason that he had no heir and left nothing behind him but a bundle of goose-quills, a notebook of white paper, three pairs of socks, some trouser buttons, and his old coat.

Into whose possession did these relics pass? Heaven only knows! The writer of this narrative has never inquired.

Akaki was wrapped in his shroud, and laid to rest in the churchyard. The great city of St Petersburg continued its life as though he had never existed. Thus disappeared a human creature who had never possessed a patron or friend, who had never elicited real hearty sympathy from anyone, nor even aroused the curiosity of the naturalists, though they are most eager to subject a rare insect to microscopic examination.

Without a complaint he had borne the scorn and contempt of his colleagues; he had proceeded on his quiet way to the grave without anything extraordinary happening to him—only towards the end of his life he had been joyfully excited by the possession of a new cloak, and had then been overthrown by misfortune.

Some days after his conversation with the Superintendent, his superior in the chancellery, where no one knew what had become of him, sent an official to his house to demand his presence. The official returned with the news that no one would see the titular councillor any more.

"Why?" asked all the clerks.

"Because he was buried four days ago."

In such a manner did Akaki's colleagues hear of his death.

The next day his place was occupied by an official of robuster fibre, a man who did not trouble to make so many fair transcripts of state documents.

. . . . . .

It seems as though Akaki's story ended here, and that there was nothing more to be said of him; but the modest titular councillor was destined to attract more notice after his death than during his life, and our tale now assumes a somewhat ghostly complexion.

One day there spread in St Petersburg the report that near the Katinka Bridge there appeared every night a spectre in a uniform like that of the chancellery officials; that he was searching for a stolen cloak, and stripped all passers-by of their cloaks without any regard for rank or title. It mattered not whether they were lined with wadding, mink, cat, otter, bear, or beaverskin; he took all he could get hold of. One of the titular councillor's former colleagues had seen the ghost, and quite clearly recognised Akaki. He ran as hard as he could and managed to escape, but had seen him shaking his fist in the distance. Everywhere it was reported that councillors, and not only titular councillors but also state-councillors, had caught serious colds in their honourable backs on account of these raids.

The police adopted all possible measures in order to get this ghost dead or alive into their power, and to inflict an exemplary punishment on him; but all their attempts were vain.

One evening, however, a sentinel succeeded in getting hold of the malefactor just as he was trying to rob a musician of his cloak. The sentinel summoned with all the force of his lungs two of his comrades, to whom he entrusted the prisoner while he sought for his snuff-box in order to bring some life again into his half-frozen nose. Probably his snuff was so strong that even a ghost could not stand it. Scarcely had the sentinel thrust a grain or two up his nostrils than the prisoner began to sneeze so violently that a kind of mist rose before the eyes of the sentinels. While the three were rubbing their eyes, the prisoner disappeared. Since that day, all the sentries were so afraid of the ghost that they did not even venture to arrest the living but shouted to them from afar "Go on! Go on!"

Meanwhile the ghost extended his depredations to the other side of the Katinka Bridge, and spread dismay and alarm in the whole of the quarter.

But now we must return to the Superintendent, who is the real origin of our fantastic yet so veracious story. First of all we must do him the justice to state that after Akaki's departure he felt a certain sympathy for him. He was by no means without a sense of justice—no, he possessed various good qualities, but his infatuation about his title hindered him from showing his good side. When his friend left him, his thoughts began to occupy themselves with the unfortunate titular councillor, and from that moment onwards he saw him constantly in his mind's eye, crushed by the severe reproof which had been administered to him. This image so haunted him that at last one day he ordered one of his officials to find out what had become of Akaki, and whether anything could be done for him.

When the messenger returned with the news that the poor man had died soon after that interview, the Superintendent felt a pang in his conscience, and remained the whole day absorbed in melancholy brooding.

In order to banish his unpleasant sensations, he went in the evening to a friend's house, where he hoped to find pleasant society and what was the chief thing, some other officials of his own rank, so that he would not be obliged to feel bored. And in fact he did succeed in throwing off his melancholy thoughts there; he unbent and became lively, took an active part in the conversation, and passed a very pleasant evening. At supper he drank two glasses of champagne, which, as everyone knows, is an effective means of heightening one's cheerfulness.

As he sat in his sledge, wrapped in his mantle, on his way home, his mind was full of pleasant reveries. He thought of the society in which he had passed such a cheerful evening, and of all the excellent jokes with which he had made them laugh. He repeated some of them to himself half-aloud, and laughed at them again.

From time to time, however, he was disturbed in this cheerful mood by violent gusts of wind, which from some corner or other blew a quantity of snowflakes into his face, lifted the folds of his cloak, and made it belly like a sail, so that he had to exert all his strength to hold it firmly on his shoulders. Suddenly he felt a powerful hand seize him by the collar. He turned round, perceived a short man in an old, shabby uniform, and recognised with terror Akaki's face, which wore a deathly pallor and emaciation.

The titular councillor opened his mouth, from which issued a kind of corpse-like odour, and with inexpressible fright the Superintendent heard him say, "At last I have you—by the collar! I need your cloak. You did not trouble about me when I was in distress; you thought it necessary to reprimand me. Now give me your cloak."

The high dignitary nearly choked. In his office, and especially in the presence of his subordinates, he was a man of imposing manners. He only needed to fix his eye on one of them and they all seemed impressed by his pompous bearing. But, as is the case with many such officials, all this was only outward show; at this moment he felt so upset that he seriously feared for his health. Taking off his cloak with a feverish, trembling hand, he handed it to Akaki, and called to his coachman, "Drive home quickly."

When the coachman heard this voice, which did not sound as it usually did, and had often been accompanied by blows of a whip, he bent his head cautiously and drove on apace.

Soon afterwards the Superintendent found himself at home. Cloakless, he retired to his room with a pale face and wild looks, and had such a bad night that on the following morning his daughter exclaimed "Father, are you ill?" But he said nothing of what he had seen, though a very deep impression had been made on him. From that day onwards he no longer addressed to his subordinates in a violent tone the words, "Do you know with whom you are speaking? Do you know who is standing before you?" Or if it ever did happen that he spoke to them in a domineering tone, it was not till he had first listened to what they had to say.

Strangely enough, from that time the spectre never appeared again. Probably it was the Superintendent's cloak which he had been seeking so earnestly; now he had it and did not want anything more. Various persons, however, asserted that this formidable ghost was still to be seen in other parts of the city. A sentinel went so far as to say that he had seen him with his own eyes glide like a furtive shadow behind a house. But this sentinel was of such a nervous disposition that he had been chaffed about his timidity more than once. Since he did not venture to seize the flitting shadow, he stole after it in the darkness; but the shadow turned round and shouted at him "What do you want?" shaking an enormous fist, such as no man had ever possessed.

"I want nothing," answered the sentry, quickly retiring.

This shadow, however, was taller than the ghost of the titular councillor, and had an enormous moustache. He went with great strides towards the Obuchoff Bridge, and disappeared in the darkness.

THE NOSE

I

On the 25th March, 18—, a very strange occurrence took place in St Petersburg. On the Ascension Avenue there lived a barber of the name of Ivan Jakovlevitch. He had lost his family name, and on his sign-board, on which was depicted the head of a gentleman with one cheek soaped, the only inscription to be read was, "Blood-letting done here."

On this particular morning he awoke pretty early. Becoming aware of the smell of fresh-baked bread, he sat up a little in bed, and saw his wife, who had a special partiality for coffee, in the act of taking some fresh-baked bread out of the oven.

"To-day, Prasskovna Ossipovna," he said, "I do not want any coffee; I should like a fresh loaf with onions."

"The blockhead may eat bread only as far as I am concerned," said his wife to herself; "then I shall have a chance of getting some coffee." And she threw a loaf on the table.

For the sake of propriety, Ivan Jakovlevitch drew a coat over his shirt, sat down at the table, shook out some salt for himself, prepared two onions, assumed a serious expression, and began to cut the bread. After he had cut the loaf in two halves, he looked, and to his great astonishment saw something whitish sticking in it. He carefully poked round it with his knife, and felt it with his finger.

"Quite firmly fixed!" he murmured in his beard. "What can it be?"

He put in his finger, and drew out—a nose!

Ivan Jakovlevitch at first let his hands fall from sheer astonishment; then he rubbed his eyes and began to feel it. A nose, an actual nose; and, moreover, it seemed to be the nose of an acquaintance! Alarm and terror were depicted in Ivan's face; but these feelings were slight in comparison with the disgust which took possession of his wife.

"Whose nose have you cut off, you monster?" she screamed, her face red with anger. "You scoundrel! You tippler! I myself will report you to the police! Such a rascal! Many customers have told me that while you were shaving them, you held them so tight by the nose that they could hardly sit still."

But Ivan Jakovlevitch was more dead than alive; he saw at once that this nose could belong to no other than to Kovaloff, a member of the Municipal Committee whom he shaved every Sunday and Wednesday.

"Stop, Prasskovna Ossipovna! I will wrap it in a piece of cloth and place it in the corner. There it may remain for the present; later on I will take it away."

"No, not there! Shall I endure an amputated nose in my room? You understand nothing except how to strop a razor. You know nothing of the duties and obligations of a respectable man. You vagabond! You good-for-nothing! Am I to undertake all responsibility for you at the police-office? Ah, you soap-smearer! You blockhead! Take it away where you like, but don't let it stay under my eyes!"

Ivan Jakovlevitch stood there flabbergasted. He thought and thought, and knew not what he thought.

"The devil knows how that happened!" he said at last, scratching his head behind his ear. "Whether I came home drunk last night or not, I really don't know; but in all probability this is a quite extraordinary occurrence, for a loaf is something baked and a nose is something different. I don't understand the matter at all." And Ivan Jakovlevitch was silent. The thought that the police might find him in unlawful possession of a nose and arrest him, robbed him of all presence of mind. Already he began to have visions of a red collar with silver braid and of a sword—and he trembled all over.

At last he finished dressing himself, and to the accompaniment of the emphatic exhortations of his spouse, he wrapped up the nose in a cloth and issued into the street.

He intended to lose it somewhere—either at somebody's door, or in a public square, or in a narrow alley; but just then, in order to complete his bad luck, he was met by an acquaintance, who showered inquiries upon him. "Hullo, Ivan Jakovlevitch! Whom are you going to shave so early in the morning?" etc., so that he could find no suitable opportunity to do what he wanted. Later on he did let the nose drop, but a sentry bore down upon him with his halberd, and said, "Look out! You have let something drop!" and Ivan Jakovlevitch was obliged to pick it up and put it in his pocket.

A feeling of despair began to take possession of him; all the more as the streets became more thronged and the merchants began to open their shops. At last he resolved to go to the Isaac Bridge, where perhaps he might succeed in throwing it into the Neva.

But my conscience is a little uneasy that I have not yet given any detailed information about Ivan Jakovlevitch, an estimable man in many ways.

Like every honest Russian tradesman, Ivan Jakovlevitch was a terrible drunkard, and although he shaved other people's faces every day, his own was always unshaved. His coat (he never wore an overcoat) was quite mottled, i.e. it had been black, but become brownish-yellow; the collar was quite shiny, and instead of the three buttons, only the threads by which they had been fastened were to be seen.

Ivan Jakovlevitch was a great cynic, and when Kovaloff, the member of the Municipal Committee, said to him, as was his custom while being shaved, "Your hands always smell, Ivan Jakovlevitch!" the latter answered, "What do they smell of?" "I don't know, my friend, but they smell very strong." Ivan Jakovlevitch after taking a pinch of snuff would then, by way of reprisals, set to work to soap him on the cheek, the upper lip, behind the ears, on the chin, and everywhere.

This worthy man now stood on the Isaac Bridge. At first he looked round him, then he leant on the railings of the bridge, as though he wished to look down and see how many fish were swimming past, and secretly threw the nose, wrapped in a little piece of cloth, into the water. He felt as though a ton weight had been lifted off him, and laughed cheerfully. Instead, however, of going to shave any officials, he turned his steps to a building, the sign-board of which bore the legend "Teas served here," in order to have a glass of punch, when suddenly he perceived at the other end of the bridge a police inspector of imposing exterior, with long whiskers, three-cornered hat, and sword hanging at his side. He nearly fainted; but the police inspector beckoned to him with his hand and said, "Come here, my dear sir."

Ivan Jakovlevitch, knowing how a gentleman should behave, took his hat off quickly, went towards the police inspector and said, "I hope you are in the best of health."

"Never mind my health. Tell me, my friend, why you were standing on the bridge."

"By heaven, gracious sir, I was on the way to my customers, and only looked down to see if the river was flowing quickly."

"That is a lie! You won't get out of it like that. Confess the truth."

"I am willing to shave Your Grace two or even three times a week gratis," answered Ivan Jakovlevitch.

"No, my friend, don't put yourself out! Three barbers are busy with me already, and reckon it a high honour that I let them show me their skill. Now then, out with it! What were you doing there?"

Ivan Jakovlevitch grew pale. But here the strange episode vanishes in mist, and what further happened is not known.

II

Kovaloff, the member of the Municipal Committee, awoke fairly early that morning, and made a droning noise— "Brr! Brr!"—through his lips, as he always did, though he could not say why. He stretched himself, and told his valet to give him a little mirror which was on the table. He wished to look at the heat-boil which had appeared on his nose the previous evening; but to his great astonishment, he saw that instead of his nose he had a perfectly smooth vacancy in his face. Thoroughly alarmed, he ordered some water to be brought, and rubbed his eyes with a towel. Sure enough, he had no longer a nose! Then he sprang out of bed, and shook himself violently! No, no nose any more! He dressed himself and went at once to the police superintendent.

But before proceeding further, we must certainly give the reader some information about Kovaloff, so that he may know what sort of a man this member of the Municipal Committee really was. These committee-men, who obtain that title by means of certificates of learning, must not be compared with the committee-men appointed for the Caucasus district, who are of quite a different kind. The learned committee-man—but Russia is such a wonderful country that when one committee-man is spoken of all the others from Riga to Kamschatka refer it to themselves. The same is also true of all other titled officials. Kovaloff had been a Caucasian committee-man two years previously, and could not forget that he had occupied that position; but in order to enhance his own importance, he never called himself "committee-man" but "Major."

"Listen, my dear," he used to say when he met an old woman in the street who sold shirt-fronts; "go to my house in Sadovaia Street and ask 'Does Major Kovaloff live here?' Any child can tell you where it is."

Accordingly we will call him for the future Major Kovaloff. It was his custom to take a daily walk on the Neffsky

Avenue. The collar of his shirt was always remarkably clean and stiff. He wore the same style of whiskers as those that are worn by governors of districts, architects, and regimental doctors; in short, all those who have full red cheeks and play a good game of whist. These whiskers grow straight across the cheek towards the nose.

Major Kovaloff wore a number of seals, on some of which were engraved armorial bearings, and others the names of the days of the week. He had come to St Petersburg with the view of obtaining some position corresponding to his rank, if possible that of vice-governor of a province; but he was prepared to be content with that of a bailiff in some department or other. He was, moreover, not disinclined to marry, but only such a lady who could bring with her a dowry of two hundred thousand roubles. Accordingly, the reader can judge for himself what his sensations were when he found in his face, instead of a fairly symmetrical nose, a broad, flat vacancy.

To increase his misfortune, not a single droshky was to be seen in the street, and so he was obliged to proceed on foot. He wrapped himself up in his cloak, and held his handkerchief to his face as though his nose bled. "But perhaps it is all only my imagination; it is impossible that a nose should drop off in such a silly way," he thought, and stepped into a confectioner's shop in order to look into the mirror.

Fortunately no customer was in the shop; only small shop-boys were cleaning it out, and putting chairs and tables straight. Others with sleepy faces were carrying fresh cakes on trays, and yesterday's newspapers stained with coffee were still lying about. "Thank God no one is here!" he said to himself. "Now I can look at myself leisurely."

He stepped gingerly up to a mirror and looked.

"What an infernal face!" he exclaimed, and spat with disgust. "If there were only something there instead of the nose, but there is absolutely nothing."

He bit his lips with vexation, left the confectioner's, and resolved, quite contrary to his habit, neither to look nor smile at anyone on the street. Suddenly he halted as if rooted to the spot before a door, where something extraordinary happened. A carriage drew up at the entrance; the carriage door was opened, and a gentleman in uniform came out and hurried up the steps. How great was Kovaloff's terror and astonishment when he saw that it was his own nose!

At this extraordinary sight, everything seemed to turn round with him. He felt as though he could hardly keep upright on his legs; but, though trembling all over as though with fever, he resolved to wait till the nose should return to the carriage. After about two minutes the nose actually came out again. It wore a gold-embroidered uniform with a stiff, high collar, trousers of chamois leather, and a sword hung at its side. The hat, adorned with a plume, showed that it held the rank of a state-councillor. It was obvious that it was paying "duty-calls." It looked round on both sides, called to the coachman "Drive on," and got into the carriage, which drove away.

Poor Kovaloff nearly lost his reason. He did not know what to think of this extraordinary procedure. And indeed how was it possible that the nose, which only yesterday he had on his face, and which could neither walk nor drive, should wear a uniform. He ran after the carriage, which fortunately had stopped a short way off before the Grand Bazar of Moscow. He hurried towards it and pressed through a crowd of beggar-women with their faces bound up, leaving only two openings for the eyes, over whom he had formerly so often made merry.

There were only a few people in front of the Bazar. Kovaloff was so agitated that he could decide on nothing, and looked for the nose everywhere. At last he saw it standing before a shop. It seemed half buried in its stiff collar, and was attentively inspecting the wares displayed.

"How can I get at it?" thought Kovaloff. "Everything— the uniform, the hat, and so on—show that it is a state-councillor. How the deuce has that happened?"

He began to cough discreetly near it, but the nose paid him not the least attention.

"Honourable sir," said Kovaloff at last, plucking up courage, "honourable sir."

"What do you want?" asked the nose, and turned round.

"It seems to me strange, most respected sir—you should know where you belong—and I find you all of a sudden—where? Judge yourself."

"Pardon me, I do not understand what you are talking about. Explain yourself more distinctly."

"How shall I make my meaning plainer to him?" Then plucking up fresh courage, he continued, "Naturally—besides I am a Major. You must admit it is not befitting that I should go about without a nose. An old apple-woman on the Ascension Bridge may carry on her business without one, but since I am on the look out for a post; besides in many houses I am acquainted with ladies of high position—Madame Tchektyriev, wife of a state-councillor, and many others. So you see—I do not know, honourable sir, what you——" (here the Major shrugged his shoulders). "Pardon me; if one regards the matter from the point of view of duty and honour—you will yourself understand——"

"I understand nothing," answered the nose. "I repeat, please explain yourself more distinctly."

"Honourable sir," said Kovaloff with dignity, "I do not know how I am to understand your words. It seems to me the matter is as clear as possible. Or do you wish—but you are after all my own nose!"

The nose looked at the Major and wrinkled its forehead. "There you are wrong, respected sir; I am myself. Besides, there can be no close relations between us. To judge by the buttons of your uniform, you must be in quite a different department to mine." So saying, the nose turned away.

Kovaloff was completely puzzled; he did not know what to do, and still less what to think. At this moment he heard the pleasant rustling of a lady's dress, and there approached an elderly lady wearing a quantity of lace, and by her side her graceful daughter in a white dress which set off her slender figure to advantage, and wearing a light straw hat. Behind the ladies marched a tall lackey with long whiskers.

Kovaloff advanced a few steps, adjusted his cambric collar, arranged his seals which hung by a little gold chain, and with smiling face fixed his eyes on the graceful lady, who bowed lightly like a spring flower, and raised to her brow her little white hand with transparent fingers. He smiled still more when he spied under the brim of her hat her little round chin, and part of her cheek faintly tinted with rose-colour. But suddenly he sprang back as though he had been scorched. He remembered that he had nothing but an absolute blank in place of a nose, and tears started to his eyes. He turned round in order to tell the gentleman in uniform that he was only a state-councillor in appearance, but really a scoundrel and a rascal, and nothing else but his own nose; but the nose was no longer there. He had had time to go, doubtless in order to continue his visits.

His disappearance plunged Kovaloff into despair. He went back and stood for a moment under a colonnade, looking round him on all sides in hope of perceiving the nose somewhere. He remembered very well that it wore a hat with a plume in it and a gold-embroidered uniform; but he had not noticed the shape of the cloak, nor the colour of the carriages and the horses, nor even whether a lackey stood behind it, and, if so, what sort of livery he wore. Moreover, so many carriages were passing that it would have been difficult to recognise one, and even if he had done so, there would have been no means of stopping it.

The day was fine and sunny. An immense crowd was passing to and fro in the Neffsky Avenue; a variegated stream of ladies flowed along the pavement. There was his acquaintance, the Privy Councillor, whom he was accustomed to style "General," especially when strangers were present. There was Iarygin, his intimate friend who always lost in the evenings at whist; and there another Major, who had obtained the rank of committee-man in the Caucasus, beckoned to him.

"Go to the deuce!" said Kovaloff *sotto voce*. "Hi! coachman, drive me straight to the superintendent of police." So saying, he got into a droshky and continued to shout all the time to the coachman "Drive hard!"

"Is the police superintendent at home?" he asked on entering the front hall.

"No, sir," answered the porter, "he has just gone out."

"Ah, just as I thought!"

"Yes," continued the porter, "he has only just gone out; if you had been a moment earlier you would perhaps have caught him."

Kovaloff, still holding his handkerchief to his face, re-entered the droshky and cried in a despairing voice "Drive on!"

"Where?" asked the coachman.

"Straight on!"

"But how? There are cross-roads here. Shall I go to the right or the left?"

This question made Kovaloff reflect. In his situation it was necessary to have recourse to the police; not because the affair had anything to do with them directly but because they acted more promptly than other authorities. As for demanding any explanation from the department to which the nose claimed to belong, it would, he felt, be useless, for the answers of that gentleman showed that he regarded nothing as sacred, and he might just as likely have lied in this matter as in saying that he had never seen Kovaloff.

But just as he was about to order the coachman to drive to the police-station, the idea occurred to him that this rascally scoundrel who, at their first meeting, had behaved so disloyally towards him, might, profiting by the delay, quit the city secretly; and then all his searching would be in vain, or might last over a whole month. Finally, as though visited with a heavenly inspiration, he resolved to go directly to an advertisement office, and to advertise the loss of his nose, giving all its distinctive characteristics in detail, so that anyone who found it might bring it at once to him, or at any rate inform him where it lived. Having decided on this course, he ordered the coachman to drive to the advertisement office, and all the way he continued to punch him in the back—"Quick, scoundrel! quick!"

"Yes, sir!" answered the coachman, lashing his shaggy horse with the reins.

At last they arrived, and Kovaloff, out of breath, rushed into a little room where a grey-haired official, in an old coat and with spectacles on his nose, sat at a table holding his pen between his teeth, counting a heap of copper coins.

"Who takes in the advertisements here?" exclaimed Kovaloff.

"At your service, sir," answered the grey-haired functionary, looking up and then fastening his eyes again on the heap of coins before him.

"I wish to place an advertisement in your paper——"

"Have the kindness to wait a minute," answered the official, putting down figures on paper with one hand, and with the other moving two balls on his calculating-frame.

A lackey, whose silver-laced coat showed that he served in one of the houses of the nobility, was standing by the table with a note in his hand, and speaking in a lively tone, by way of showing himself sociable. "Would you believe it, sir, this little dog is really not worth twenty-four kopecks, and for my own part I would not give a farthing for it; but the countess is quite gone upon it, and offers a hundred roubles' reward to anyone who finds it. To tell you the truth, the tastes of these people are very different from ours; they don't mind giving five hundred or a thousand roubles for a poodle or a pointer, provided it be a good one."

The official listened with a serious air while counting the number of letters contained in the note. At either side of the table stood a number of housekeepers, clerks and porters, carrying notes. The writer of one wished to sell a barouche, which had been brought from Paris in 1814 and had been very little used; others wanted to dispose of a strong droshky which wanted one spring, a spirited horse seventeen years old, and so on. The room where these people were collected was very small, and the air was very close; but Kovaloff was not affected by it, for he had covered his face with a handkerchief, and because his nose itself was heaven knew where.

"Sir, allow me to ask you—I am in a great hurry," he said at last impatiently.

"In a moment! In a moment! Two roubles, twenty-four kopecks—one minute! One rouble, sixty-four kopecks!" said the grey-haired official, throwing their notes back to the housekeepers and porters. "What do you wish?" he said, turning to Kovaloff.

"I wish—" answered the latter, "I have just been swindled and cheated, and I cannot get hold of the perpetrator. I only want you to insert an advertisement to say that whoever brings this scoundrel to me will be well rewarded."

"What is your name, please?"

"Why do you want my name? I have many lady friends—Madame Tchektyriev, wife of a state-councillor, Madame Podtotchina, wife of a Colonel. Heaven forbid that they should get to hear of it. You can simply write 'committee-man,' or, better, 'Major.'"

"And the man who has run away is your serf."

"Serf! If he was, it would not be such a great swindle! It is the nose which has absconded."

"H'm! What a strange name. And this Mr Nose has stolen from you a considerable sum?"

"Mr Nose! Ah, you don't understand me! It is my own nose which has gone, I don't know where. The devil has played a trick on me."

"How has it disappeared? I don't understand."

"I can't tell you how, but the important point is that now it walks about the city itself a state-councillor. That is why I want you to advertise that whoever gets hold of it should bring it as soon as possible to me. Consider; how can I live without such a prominent part of my body? It is not as if it were merely a little toe; I would only have to put my foot in my boot and no one would notice its absence. Every Thursday I call on the wife of M. Tchektyriev, the state-councillor; Madame Podtotchina, a Colonel's wife who has a very pretty daughter, is one of my acquaintances; and what am I to do now? I cannot appear before them like this."

The official compressed his lips and reflected. "No, I cannot insert an advertisement like that," he said after a long pause.

"What! Why not?"

"Because it might compromise the paper. Suppose everyone could advertise that his nose was lost. People already say that all sorts of nonsense and lies are inserted."

"But this is not nonsense! There is nothing of that sort in my case."

"You think so? Listen a minute. Last week there was a case very like it. An official came, just as you have done, bringing an advertisement for the insertion of which he paid two roubles, sixty-three kopecks; and this advertisement simply announced the loss of a black-haired poodle. There did not seem to be anything out of the way in it, but it was really a satire; by the poodle was meant the cashier of some establishment or other."

"But I am not talking of a poodle, but my own nose; i.e. almost myself."

"No, I cannot insert your advertisement."

"But my nose really has disappeared!"

"That is a matter for a doctor. There are said to be people who can provide you with any kind of nose you like. But I see that you are a witty man, and like to have your little joke."

"But I swear to you on my word of honour. Look at my face yourself."

"Why put yourself out?" continued the official, taking a pinch of snuff. "All the same, if you don't mind," he added with a touch of curiosity, "I should like to have a look at it."

The committee-man removed the handkerchief from before his face.

"It certainly does look odd," said the official. "It is perfectly flat like a freshly fried pancake. It is hardly credible."

"Very well. Are you going to hesitate any more? You see it is impossible to refuse to advertise my loss. I shall be particularly obliged to you, and I shall be glad that this incident has procured me the pleasure of making your acquaintance." The Major, we see, did not even shrink from a slight humiliation.

"It certainly is not difficult to advertise it," replied the official; "but I don't see what good it would do you. However, if you lay so much stress on it, you should apply to someone who has a skilful pen, so that he may describe it as a curious, natural freak, and publish the article in the *Northern Bee*" (here he took another pinch) "for the benefit of youthful readers" (he wiped his nose), "or simply as a matter worthy of arousing public curiosity."

The committee-man felt completely discouraged. He let his eyes fall absent-mindedly on a daily paper in which theatrical performances were advertised. Reading there the name of an actress whom he knew to be pretty, he involuntarily smiled, and his hand sought his pocket to see if he had a blue ticket—for in Kovaloff's opinion superior officers like himself should not take a lesser-priced seat; but the thought of his lost nose suddenly spoilt everything.

The official himself seemed touched at his difficult position. Desiring to console him, he tried to express his sympathy by a few polite words. "I much regret," he said, "your extraordinary mishap. Will you not try a pinch of snuff? It clears the head, banishes depression, and is a good preventive against hæmorrhoids."

So saying, he reached his snuff-box out to Kovaloff, skilfully concealing at the same time the cover, which was adorned with the portrait of some lady or other.

This act, quite innocent in itself, exasperated Kovaloff. "I don't understand what you find to joke about in the matter," he exclaimed angrily. "Don't you see that I lack precisely the essential feature for taking snuff? The devil take your snuff-box. I don't want to look at snuff now, not even the best, certainly not your vile stuff!"

So saying, he left the advertisement office in a state of profound irritation, and went to the commissary of police. He arrived just as this dignitary was reclining on his couch, and saying to himself with a sigh of satisfaction, "Yes, I shall make a nice little sum out of that."

It might be expected, therefore, that the committee-man's visit would be quite inopportune.

This police commissary was a great patron of all the arts and industries; but what he liked above everything else was a cheque. "It is a thing," he used to say, "to which it is not easy to find an equivalent; it requires no food, it does not take up much room, it stays in one's pocket, and if it falls, it is not broken."

The commissary accorded Kovaloff a fairly frigid reception, saying that the afternoon was not the best time to come with a case, that nature required one to rest a little after eating (this showed the committee-man that the commissary was acquainted with the aphorisms of the ancient sages), and that respectable people did not have their noses stolen.

The last allusion was too direct. We must remember that Kovaloff was a very sensitive man. He did not mind anything said against him as an individual, but he could not endure any reflection on his rank or social position. He even believed that in comedies one might allow attacks on junior officers, but never on their seniors.

The commissary's reception of him hurt his feelings so much that he raised his head proudly, and said with dignity, "After such insulting expressions on your part, I have nothing more to say." And he left the place.

He reached his house quite wearied out. It was already growing dark. After all his fruitless search, his room seemed to him melancholy and even ugly. In the vestibule he saw his valet Ivan stretched on the leather couch and amusing himself by spitting at the ceiling, which he did very cleverly, hitting every time the same spot. His servant's equanimity enraged him; he struck him on the forehead with his hat, and said, "You good-for-nothing, you are always playing the fool!"

Ivan rose quickly and hastened to take off his master's cloak.

Once in his room, the Major, tired and depressed, threw himself in an armchair and, after sighing a while, began to soliloquise:

"In heaven's name, why should such a misfortune befall me? If I had lost an arm or a leg, it would be less insupportable; but a man without a nose! Devil take it!—what is he good for? He is only fit to be thrown out of the window. If it had been taken from me in war or in a duel, or if I had lost it by my own fault! But it has disappeared inexplicably. But no! it is impossible," he continued after reflecting a few moments, "it is incredible that a nose can disappear like that—quite incredible. I must be dreaming, or suffering from some hallucination; perhaps I swallowed, by mistake instead of water, the brandy with which I rub my chin after being shaved. That fool of an Ivan must have forgotten to take it away, and I must have swallowed it."

In order to find out whether he were really drunk, the Major pinched himself so hard that he unvoluntarily uttered a cry. The pain convinced him that he was quite wide awake. He walked slowly to the looking-glass and at first closed his eyes, hoping to see his nose suddenly in its proper place; but on opening them, he started back. "What a hideous sight!" he exclaimed.

It was really incomprehensible. One might easily lose a button, a silver spoon, a watch, or something similar; but a loss like this, and in one's own dwelling!

After considering all the circumstances, Major Kovaloff felt inclined to suppose that the cause of all his trouble should be laid at the door of Madame Podtotchina, the Colonel's wife, who wished him to marry her daughter. He himself paid her court readily, but always avoided coming to the point. And when the lady one day told him point-blank that she wished him to marry her daughter, he gently drew back, declaring that he was still too young, and that he had to serve five years more before he would be forty-two. This must be the reason why the lady, in revenge, had resolved to bring him into disgrace, and had hired two sorceresses for that object. One thing was certain—his nose had not been cut off; no one had entered his room, and as for Ivan Jakovlevitch—he had been shaved by him on Wednesday, and during that day and the whole of Thursday his nose had been there, as he knew and well remembered. Moreover, if his nose had been cut off he would naturally have felt pain, and doubtless the wound would not have healed so quickly, nor would the surface have been as flat as a pancake.

All kinds of plans passed through his head: should he bring a legal action against the wife of a superior officer, or should he go to her and charge her openly with her treachery?

His reflections were interrupted by a sudden light, which shone through all the chinks of the door, showing that Ivan had lit the wax-candles in the vestibule. Soon Ivan himself came in with the lights. Kovaloff quickly seized a handkerchief and covered the place where his nose had been the evening before, so that his blockhead of a servant might not gape with his mouth wide open when he saw his master's extraordinary appearance.

Scarcely had Ivan returned to the vestibule than a stranger's voice was heard there.

"Does Major Kovaloff live here?" it asked.

"Come in!" said the Major, rising rapidly and opening the door.

He saw a police official of pleasant appearance, with grey whiskers and fairly full cheeks—the same who at the commencement of this story was standing at the end of the Isaac Bridge. "You have lost your nose?" he asked.

"Exactly so."

"It has just been found."

"What—do you say?" stammered Major Kovaloff.

Joy had suddenly paralysed his tongue. He stared at the police commissary on whose cheeks and full lips fell the flickering light of the candle.

"How was it?" he asked at last.

"By a very singular chance. It has been arrested just as it was getting into a carriage for Riga. Its passport had been made out some time ago in the name of an official; and what is still more strange, I myself took it at first for a gentleman. Fortunately I had my glasses with me, and then I saw at once that it was a nose. I am shortsighted, you know, and as you stand before me I cannot distinguish your nose, your beard, or anything else. My mother-in-law can hardly see at all."

Kovaloff was beside himself with excitement. "Where is it? Where? I will hasten there at once."

"Don't put yourself out. Knowing that you need it, I have brought it with me. Another singular thing is that the principal culprit in the matter is a scoundrel of a barber living in the Ascension Avenue, who is now safely locked up. I had long suspected him of drunkenness and theft; only the day before yesterday he stole some buttons in a shop. Your nose is quite uninjured." So saying, the police commissary put his hand in his pocket and brought out the nose wrapped up in paper.

"Yes, yes, that is it!" exclaimed Kovaloff. "Will you not stay and drink a cup of tea with me?"

"I should like to very much, but I cannot. I must go at once to the House of Correction. The cost of living is very high nowadays. My mother-in-law lives with me, and there are several children; the eldest is very hopeful and intelligent, but I have no means for their education."

After the commissary's departure, Kovaloff remained for some time plunged in a kind of vague reverie, and did not recover full consciousness for several moments, so great was the effect of this unexpected good news. He placed the recovered nose carefully in the palm of his hand, and examined it again with the greatest attention.

"Yes, this is it!" he said to himself. "Here is the heat-boil on the left side, which came out yesterday." And he nearly laughed aloud with delight.

But nothing is permanent in this world. Joy in the second moment of its arrival is already less keen than in the first, is still fainter in the third, and finishes by coalescing with our normal mental state, just as the circles which the fall of a pebble forms on the surface of water, gradually die away. Kovaloff began to meditate, and saw that his difficulties were not yet over; his nose had been recovered, but it had to be joined on again in its proper place.

And suppose it could not? As he put this question to himself, Kovaloff grew pale. With a feeling of indescribable dread, he rushed towards his dressing-table, and stood before the mirror in order that he might not place his nose crookedly. His hands trembled.

Very carefully he placed it where it had been before. Horror! It did not remain there. He held it to his mouth and warmed it a little with his breath, and then placed it there again; but it would not hold.

"Hold on, you stupid!" he said.

But the nose seemed to be made of wood, and fell back on the table with a strange noise, as though it had been a cork. The Major's face began to twitch feverishly. "Is it possible that it won't stick?" he asked himself, full of alarm. But however often he tried, all his efforts were in vain.

He called Ivan, and sent him to fetch the doctor who occupied the finest flat in the mansion. This doctor was a man of imposing appearance, who had magnificent black whiskers and a healthy wife. He ate fresh apples every morning, and cleaned his teeth with extreme care, using five different tooth-brushes for three-quarters of an hour daily.

The doctor came immediately. After having asked the Major when this misfortune had happened, he raised his chin and gave him a fillip with his finger just where the nose had been, in such a way that the Major suddenly threw back his head and struck the wall with it. The doctor said that did not matter; then, making him turn his face to the right, he felt the vacant place and said "H'm!" then he made him turn it to the left and did the same; finally he again gave him a fillip with his finger, so that the Major started like a horse whose teeth are being examined. After this experiment, the doctor shook his head and said, "No, it cannot be done. Rather remain as you are, lest something worse happen. Certainly one could replace it at once, but I assure you the remedy would be worse than the disease."

"All very fine, but how am I to go on without a nose?" answered Kovaloff. "There is nothing worse than that. How can I show myself with such a villainous appearance? I go into good society, and this evening I am invited to two parties. I know several ladies, Madame Tchektyriev, the wife of a state-councillor, Madame Podtotchina—although after what she has done, I don't want to have anything to do with her except through the agency of the police. I beg you," continued Kovaloff in a supplicating tone, "find some way or other of replacing it; even if it is not quite firm, as long as it holds at all; I can keep it in place sometimes with my hand, whenever there is any risk. Besides, I do not even dance, so that it is not likely to be injured by any sudden movement. As to your fee, be in no anxiety about that; I can well afford it."

"Believe me," answered the doctor in a voice which was neither too high nor too low, but soft and almost magnetic, "I do not treat patients from love of gain. That would be contrary to my principles and to my art. It is true that I accept fees, but that is only not to hurt my patients' feelings by refusing them. I could certainly replace your nose, but I assure you on my word of honour, it would only make matters worse. Rather let Nature do her own work. Wash the place often with cold water, and I assure you that even without a nose, you will be just as well as if you had one. As to the nose itself, I advise you to have it preserved in a bottle of spirits, or, still better, of warm vinegar mixed with two spoonfuls of brandy, and then you can sell it at a good price. I would be willing to take it myself, provided you do not ask too much."

"No, no, I shall not sell it at any price. I would rather it were lost again."

"Excuse me," said the doctor, taking his leave. "I hoped to be useful to you, but I can do nothing more; you are at any rate convinced of my good-will." So saying, the doctor left the room with a dignified air.

Kovaloff did not even notice his departure. Absorbed in a profound reverie, he only saw the edge of his snow-white cuffs emerging from the sleeves of his black coat.

The next day he resolved, before bringing a formal action, to write to the Colonel's wife and see whether she would not return to him, without further dispute, that of which she had deprived him.

The letter ran as follows:

"To Madame Alexandra Podtotchina,

"I hardly understand your method of action. Be sure that by adopting such a course you will gain nothing, and will certainly not succeed in making me marry your daughter. Believe me, the story of my nose has become well known; it is you and no one else who have taken the principal part in it. Its unexpected separation from the place which it occupied, its flight and its appearances sometimes in the disguise of an official, sometimes in proper person, are nothing but the consequence of unholy spells employed by you or by persons who, like you, are addicted to such honourable pursuits. On my part, I wish to inform you, that if the above-mentioned nose is not restored to-day to its proper place, I shall be obliged to have recourse to legal procedure.

"For the rest, with all respect, I have the honour to be your humble servant,

"Platon Kovaloff."

The reply was not long in coming, and was as follows:

"Major Platon Kovaloff,—

"Your letter has profoundly astonished me. I must confess that I had not expected such unjust reproaches on your part. I assure you that the official of whom you speak has not been at my house, either disguised or in his proper person. It is true that Philippe Ivanovitch Potantchikoff has paid visits at my house, and though he has actually asked for my daughter's hand, and was a man of good breeding, respectable and intelligent, I never gave him any hope.

"Again, you say something about a nose. If you intend to imply by that that I wished to snub you, i.e. to meet you with a refusal, I am very astonished because, as you well know, I was quite of the opposite mind. If after this you wish to ask for my daughter's hand, I should be glad to gratify you, for such has also been the object of my most fervent desire, in the hope of the accomplishment of which, I remain, yours most sincerely,

"Alexandra Podtotchina."

"No," said Kovaloff, after having reperused the letter, "she is certainly not guilty. It is impossible. Such a letter could not be written by a criminal." The committee-man was experienced in such matters, for he had been often officially deputed to conduct criminal investigations while in the Caucasus. "But then how and by what trick of fate has the thing happened?" he said to himself with a gesture of discouragement. "The devil must be at the bottom of it."

Meanwhile the rumour of this extraordinary event had spread all over the city, and, as is generally the case, not without numerous additions. At that period there was a general disposition to believe in the miraculous; the public had recently been impressed by experiments in magnetism. The story of the floating chairs in Koniouchennaia Street was still quite recent, and there was nothing astonishing in hearing soon afterwards that Major Kovaloff's nose was to be seen walking every day at three o'clock on the Neffsky Avenue. The crowd of curious spectators which gathered there daily was enormous. On one occasion someone spread a report that the nose was in Junker's stores and immediately the place was besieged by such a crowd that the police had to interfere and establish order. A certain speculator with a grave, whiskered face, who sold cakes at a theatre door, had some strong wooden benches made which he placed before the window of the stores, and obligingly invited the public to stand on them and look in, at the modest charge of twenty-four kopecks. A veteran colonel, leaving his house earlier than usual expressly for the purpose, had the greatest difficulty in elbowing his way through the crowd, but to his great indignation he saw nothing in the store window but an ordinary flannel waistcoat and a coloured lithograph representing a young girl darning a stocking, while an elegant youth in a waistcoat with large lappels watched her from behind a tree. The picture had hung in the same place for more than ten years. The colonel went off, growling savagely to himself, "How can the fools let themselves be excited by such idiotic stories?"

Then another rumour got abroad, to the effect that the nose of Major Kovaloff was in the habit of walking not on the Neffsky Avenue but in the Tauris Gardens. Some students of the Academy of Surgery went there on purpose to see it. A high-born lady wrote to the keeper of the gardens asking him to show her children this rare phenomenon, and to give them some suitable instruction on the occasion.

All these incidents were eagerly collected by the town wits, who just then were very short of anecdotes adapted to amuse ladies. On the other hand, the minority of solid, sober people were very much displeased. One gentleman asserted with great indignation that he could not understand how in our enlightened age such absurdities could spread abroad, and he was astonished that the Government did not direct their attention to the matter. This gentleman evidently belonged to the category of those people who wish the Government to interfere in everything, even in their daily quarrels with their wives.

But here the course of events is again obscured by a veil.

III

Strange events happen in this world, events which are sometimes entirely improbable. The same nose which had masqueraded as a state-councillor, and caused so much sensation in the town, was found one morning in its proper place, i.e. between the cheeks of Major Kovaloff, as if nothing had happened.

This occurred on 7th April. On awaking, the Major looked by chance into a mirror and perceived a nose. He quickly put his hand to it; it was there beyond a doubt!

"Oh!" exclaimed Kovaloff. For sheer joy he was on the point of performing a dance barefooted across his room, but the entrance of Ivan prevented him. He told him to bring water, and after washing himself, he looked again in the glass. The nose was there! Then he dried his face with a towel and looked again. Yes, there was no mistake about it!

"Look here, Ivan, it seems to me that I have a heat-boil on my nose," he said to his valet.

And he thought to himself at the same time, "That will be a nice business if Ivan says to me 'No, sir, not only is there no boil, but your nose itself is not there!'"

But Ivan answered, "There is nothing, sir; I can see no boil on your nose."

"Good! Good!" exclaimed the Major, and snapped his fingers with delight.

At this moment the barber, Ivan Jakovlevitch, put his head in at the door, but as timidly as a cat which has just been beaten for stealing lard.

"Tell me first, are your hands clean?" asked Kovaloff when he saw him.

"Yes, sir."

"You lie."

"I swear they are perfectly clean, sir."

"Very well; then come here."

Kovaloff seated himself. Jakovlevitch tied a napkin under his chin, and in the twinkling of an eye covered his beard and part of his cheeks with a copious creamy lather.

"There it is!" said the barber to himself, as he glanced at the nose. Then he bent his head a little and examined it from one side. "Yes, it actually is the nose—really, when one thinks——" he continued, pursuing his mental soliloquy and still looking at it. Then quite gently, with infinite precaution, he raised two fingers in the air in order to take hold of it by the extremity, as he was accustomed to do.

"Now then, take care!" Kovaloff exclaimed.

Ivan Jakovlevitch let his arm fall and felt more embarrassed than he had ever done in his life. At last he began to pass the razor very lightly over the Major's chin, and although it was very difficult to shave him without using the olfactory organ as a point of support, he succeeded, however, by placing his wrinkled thumb against the Major's lower jaw

92

and cheek, thus overcoming all obstacles and bringing his task to a safe conclusion.

When the barber had finished, Kovaloff hastened to dress himself, took a droshky, and drove straight to the confectioner's. As he entered it, he ordered a cup of chocolate. He then stepped straight to the mirror; the nose was there!

He returned joyfully, and regarded with a satirical expression two officers who were in the shop, one of whom possessed a nose not much larger than a waistcoat button.

After that he went to the office of the department where he had applied for the post of vice-governor of a province or Government bailiff. As he passed through the hall of reception, he cast a glance at the mirror; the nose was there! Then he went to pay a visit to another committee-man, a very sarcastic personage, to whom he was accustomed to say in answer to his raillery, "Yes, I know, you are the funniest fellow in St Petersburg."

On the way he said to himself, "If the Major does not burst into laughter at the sight of me, that is a most certain sign that everything is in its accustomed place."

But the Major said nothing. "Very good!" thought Kovaloff.

As he returned, he met Madame Podtotchina with her daughter. He accosted them, and they responded very graciously. The conversation lasted a long time, during which he took more than one pinch of snuff, saying to himself,

"No, you haven't caught me yet, coquettes that you are! And as to the daughter, I shan't marry her at all."

After that, the Major resumed his walks on the Neffsky Avenue and his visits to the theatre as if nothing had happened. His nose also remained in its place as if it had never quitted it. From that time he was always to be seen smiling, in a good humour, and paying attentions to pretty girls.

IV

Such was the occurrence which took place in the northern capital of our vast empire. On considering the account carefully we see that there is a good deal which looks improbable about it. Not to speak of the strange disappearance of the nose, and its appearance in different places under the disguise of a councillor of state, how was it that Kovaloff did not understand that one cannot decently advertise for a lost nose? I do not mean to say that he would have had to pay too much for the advertisement—that is a mere trifle, and I am not one of those who attach too much importance to money; but to advertise in such a case is not proper nor befitting.

Another difficulty is—how was the nose found in the baked loaf, and how did Ivan Jakovlevitch himself—no, I don't understand it at all!

But the most incomprehensible thing of all is, how authors can choose such subjects for their stories. That really surpasses my understanding. In the first place, no advantage results from it for the country; and in the second place, no harm results either.

All the same, when one reflects well, there really is something in the matter. Whatever may be said to the contrary, such cases do occur—rarely, it is true, but now and then actually.

MEMOIRS OF A MADMAN

October 3rd.—A strange occurrence has taken place to-day. I got up fairly late, and when Mawra brought me my clean boots, I asked her how late it was. When I heard it had long struck ten, I dressed as quickly as possible.

To tell the truth, I would rather not have gone to the office at all to-day, for I know beforehand that our department-chief will look as sour as vinegar. For some time past he has been in the habit of saying to me, "Look here, my friend; there is something wrong with your head. You often rush about as though you were possessed. Then you make such confused abstracts of the documents that the devil himself cannot make them out; you write the title without any capital letters, and add neither the date nor the docket-number." The long-legged scoundrel! He is certainly envious of me, because I sit in the director's work-room, and mend His Excellency's pens. In a word, I should not have gone to the office if I had not hoped to meet the accountant, and perhaps squeeze a little advance out of this skinflint.

A terrible man, this accountant! As for his advancing one's salary once in a way—you might sooner expect the skies to fall. You may beg and beseech him, and be on the very verge of ruin—this grey devil won't budge an inch. At the same time, his own cook at home, as all the world knows, boxes his ears.

I really don't see what good one gets by serving in our department. There are no plums there. In the fiscal and judicial offices it is quite different. There some ungainly fellow sits in a corner and writes and writes; he has such a shabby coat and such an ugly mug that one would like to spit on both of them. But you should see what a splendid country-house he has rented. He would not condescend to accept a gilt porcelain cup as a present. "You can give that to your family doctor," he would say. Nothing less than a pair of chestnut horses, a fine carriage, or a beaver-fur coat worth three hundred roubles would be good enough for him. And yet he seems so mild and quiet, and asks so amiably, "Please lend me your penknife; I wish to mend my pen." Nevertheless, he knows how to scarify a petitioner till he has hardly a whole stitch left on his body.

In our office it must be admitted everything is done in a proper and gentlemanly way; there is more cleanness and elegance than one will ever find in Government offices. The tables are mahogany, and everyone is addressed as "sir." And truly, were it not for this official propriety, I should long ago have sent in my resignation.

I put on my old cloak, and took my umbrella, as a light rain was falling. No one was to be seen on the streets except some women, who had flung their skirts over their heads.

Here and there one saw a cabman or a shopman with his umbrella up. Of the higher classes one only saw an official here and there. One I saw at the street-crossing, and thought to myself, "Ah! my friend, you are not going to the office, but after that young lady who walks in front of you. You are just like the officers who run after every petticoat they see."

As I was thus following the train of my thoughts, I saw a carriage stop before a shop just as I was passing it. I recognised it at once; it was our director's carriage. "He has nothing to do in the shop," I said to myself; "it must be his daughter."

I pressed myself close against the wall. A lackey opened the carriage door, and, as I had expected, she fluttered like a bird out of it. How proudly she looked right and left; how she drew her eyebrows together, and shot lightnings from her eyes—good heavens! I am lost, hopelessly lost!

But why must she come out in such abominable weather? And yet they say women are so mad on their finery!

She did not recognise me. I had wrapped myself as closely as possible in my cloak. It was dirty and old-fashioned, and I would not have liked to have been seen by her wearing it. Now they wear cloaks with long collars, but mine has only a short double collar, and the cloth is of inferior quality.

Her little dog could not get into the shop, and remained outside. I know this dog; its name is "Meggy."

Before I had been standing there a minute, I heard a voice call, "Good day, Meggy!"

Who the deuce was that? I looked round and saw two ladies hurrying by under an umbrella—one old, the other fairly young. They had already passed me when I heard the same voice say again, "For shame, Meggy!"

What was that? I saw Meggy sniffing at a dog which ran behind the ladies. The deuce! I thought to myself, "I am not drunk? That happens pretty seldom."

"No, Fidel, you are wrong," I heard Meggy say quite distinctly. "I was—bow—wow!—I was—bow! wow! wow!—very ill."

What an extraordinary dog! I was, to tell the truth, quite amazed to hear it talk human language. But when I considered the matter well, I ceased to be astonished. In fact, such things have already happened in the world. It is said that in England a fish put its head out of water and said a word or two in such an extraordinary language that learned men have been puzzling over them for three years, and have not succeeded in interpreting them yet. I also read in the paper of two cows who entered a shop and asked for a pound of tea.

Meanwhile what Meggy went on to say seemed to me still more remarkable. She added, "I wrote to you lately, Fidel; perhaps Polkan did not bring you the letter."

Now I am willing to forfeit a whole month's salary if I ever heard of dogs writing before. This has certainly astonished me. For some little time past I hear and see things which no other man has heard and seen.

"I will," I thought, "follow that dog in order to get to the bottom of the matter. Accordingly, I opened my umbrella and went after the two ladies. They went down Bean Street, turned through Citizen Street and Carpenter Street, and finally halted on the Cuckoo Bridge before a large house. I know this house; it is Sverkoff's. What a monster he is! What sort of people live there! How many cooks, how many bagmen! There are brother officials of mine also there packed on each other like herrings. And I have a friend there, a fine player on the cornet."

The ladies mounted to the fifth story. "Very good," thought I; "I will make a note of the number, in order to follow up the matter at the first opportunity."

October 4th.—To-day is Wednesday, and I was as usual in the office. I came early on purpose, sat down, and mended all the pens.

Our director must be a very clever man. The whole room is full of bookcases. I read the titles of some of the books; they were very learned, beyond the comprehension of people of my class, and all in French and German. I look at his face; see! how much dignity there is in his eyes. I never hear a single superfluous word from his mouth, except that when he hands over the documents, he asks "What sort of weather is it?"

No, he is not a man of our class; he is a real statesman. I have already noticed that I am a special favourite of his. If now his daughter also—ah! what folly—let me say no more about it!

I have read the *Northern Bee*. What foolish people the French are! By heavens! I should like to tackle them all, and give them a thrashing. I have also read a fine description of a ball given by a landowner of Kursk. The landowners of Kursk write a fine style.

Then I noticed that it was already half-past twelve, and the director had not yet left his bedroom. But about half-past one something happened which no pen can describe.

The door opened. I thought it was the director; I jumped up with my documents from the seat, and—then—she—herself—came into the room. Ye saints! how beautifully she was dressed. Her garments were whiter than a swan's plumage—oh how splendid! A sun, indeed, a real sun!

She greeted me and asked, "Has not my father come yet?"

Ah! what a voice. A canary bird! A real canary bird!

"Your Excellency," I wanted to exclaim, "don't have me executed, but if it must be done, then kill me rather with your own angelic hand." But, God knows why, I could not bring it out, so I only said, "No, he has not come yet."

She glanced at me, looked at the books, and let her handkerchief fall. Instantly I started up, but slipped on the infernal polished floor, and nearly broke my nose. Still I succeeded in picking up the handkerchief. Ye heavenly choirs, what a handkerchief! So tender and soft, of the finest cambric. It had the scent of a general's rank!

She thanked me, and smiled so amiably that her sugar lips nearly melted. Then she left the room.

After I had sat there about an hour, a flunkey came in and said, "You can go home, Mr Ivanovitch; the director has already gone out!"

I cannot stand these lackeys! They hang about the vestibules, and scarcely vouchsafe to greet one with a nod. Yes, sometimes it is even worse; once one of these rascals offered me his snuff-box without even getting up from his chair. "Don't you know then, you country-bumpkin, that I am an official and of aristocratic birth?"

This time, however, I took my hat and overcoat quietly; these people naturally never think of helping one on with it. I went home, lay a good while on the bed, and wrote some verses in my note:

"'Tis an hour since I saw thee,
And it seems a whole long year;
If I loathe my own existence,
How can I live on, my dear?"
I think they are by Pushkin.

102

In the evening I wrapped myself in my cloak, hastened to the director's house, and waited there a long time to see if she would come out and get into the carriage. I only wanted to see her once, but she did not come.

November 6th.—Our chief clerk has gone mad. When I came to the office to-day he called me to his room and began as follows: "Look here, my friend, what wild ideas have got into your head?"

"How! What? None at all," I answered.

"Consider well. You are already past forty; it is quite time to be reasonable. What do you imagine? Do you think I don't know all your tricks? Are you trying to pay court to the director's daughter? Look at yourself and realise what you are! A nonentity, nothing else. I would not give a kopeck for you. Look well in the glass. How can you have such thoughts with such a caricature of a face?"

May the devil take him! Because his own face has a certain resemblance to a medicine-bottle, because he has a curly bush of hair on his head, and sometimes combs it upwards, and sometimes plasters it down in all kinds of queer ways, he thinks that he can do everything. I know well, I know why he is angry with me. He is envious; perhaps he has noticed the tokens of favour which have been graciously shown me. But why should I bother about him? A councillor! What sort of important animal is that? He wears a gold chain with his watch, buys himself boots at thirty roubles a pair; may the deuce take him! Am I a tailor's son or some other obscure cabbage? I am a nobleman! I can also work my way up. I am just forty-two—an age when a man's real career generally begins. Wait a bit, my friend! I too may get to a superior's rank; or perhaps, if God is gracious, even to a higher one. I shall make a name which will far outstrip yours. You think there are no able men except yourself? I only need to order a fashionable coat and wear a tie like yours, and you would be quite eclipsed.

But I have no money—that is the worst part of it!

November 8th.—I was at the theatre. "The Russian House-Fool" was performed. I laughed heartily. There was also a kind of musical comedy which contained amusing hits at barristers. The language was very broad; I wonder the censor passed it. In the comedy lines occur which accuse the merchants of cheating; their sons are said to lead immoral lives, and to behave very disrespectfully towards the nobility.

The critics also are criticised; they are said only to be able to find fault, so that authors have to beg the public for protection.

Our modern dramatists certainly write amusing things. I am very fond of the theatre. If I have only a kopeck in my pocket, I always go there. Most of my fellow-officials are uneducated boors, and never enter a theatre unless one throws free tickets at their head.

One actress sang divinely. I thought also of—but silence!

November 9th.—About eight o'clock I went to the office. The chief clerk pretended not to notice my arrival. I for my part also behaved as though he were not in existence. I read through and collated documents. About four o'clock I left. I passed by the director's house, but no one was to be seen. After dinner I lay for a good while on the bed.

November 11th.—To-day I sat in the director's room, mended twenty-three pens for him, and for Her—for Her Excellence, his daughter, four more.

The director likes to see many pens lying on his table. What a head he must have! He continually wraps himself in silence, but I don't think the smallest trifle escapes his eye. I should like to know what he is generally thinking of, what is really going on in this brain; I should like to get acquainted with the whole manner of life of these gentlemen, and get a closer view of their cunning courtiers' arts, and all the activities of these circles. I have often thought of asking His Excellence about them; but—the deuce knows why!—every time my tongue failed me and I could get nothing out but my meteorological report.

I wish I could get a look into the spare-room whose door I so often see open. And a second small room behind the spare-room excites my curiosity. How splendidly it is fitted up; what a quantity of mirrors and choice china it contains!

I should also like to cast a glance into those regions where Her Excellency, the daughter, wields the sceptre. I should like to see how all the scent-bottles and boxes are arranged in her boudoir, and the flowers which exhale so delicious a scent that one is half afraid to breathe. And her clothes lying about which are too ethereal to be called clothes—but silence!

To-day there came to me what seemed a heavenly inspiration. I remembered the conversation between the two dogs which I had overheard on the Nevski Prospect. "Very good," I thought; "now I see my way clear. I must get hold of the correspondence which these two silly dogs have carried on with each other. In it I shall probably find many things explained."

I had already once called Meggy to me and said to her, "Listen, Meggy! Now we are alone together; if you like, I will also shut the door so that no one can see us. Tell me now all that you know about your mistress. I swear to you that I will tell no one."

But the cunning dog drew in its tail, ruffled up its hair, and went quite quietly out of the door, as though it had heard nothing.

I had long been of the opinion that dogs are much cleverer than men. I also believed that they could talk, and that only a certain obstinacy kept them from doing so. They are especially watchful animals, and nothing escapes their observation. Now, cost what it may, I will go to-morrow to Sverkoff's house in order to ask after Fidel, and if I have luck, to get hold of all the letters which Meggy has written to her.

November 12th.—To-day about two o'clock in the afternoon I started in order, by some means or other, to see Fidel and question her.

I cannot stand this smell of Sauerkraut which assails one's olfactory nerves from all the shops in Citizen Street. There also exhales such an odour from under each house door, that one must hold one's nose and pass by quickly. There ascends also so much smoke and soot from the artisans' shops that it is almost impossible to get through it.

When I had climbed up to the sixth story, and had rung the bell, a rather pretty girl with a freckled face came out. I recognised her as the companion of the old lady. She blushed a little and asked "What do you want?"

"I want to have a little conversation with your dog."

She was a simple-minded girl, as I saw at once. The dog came running and barking loudly. I wanted to take hold of it, but the abominable beast nearly caught hold of my nose with its teeth. But in a corner of the room I saw its sleeping-basket. Ah! that was what I wanted. I went to it, rummaged in the straw, and to my great satisfaction drew out a little packet of small pieces of paper. When the hideous little dog saw this, it first bit me in the calf of the leg, and then, as soon as it had become aware of my theft, it began to whimper and to fawn on me; but I said, "No, you little beast; good-bye!" and hastened away.

I believe the girl thought me mad; at any rate she was thoroughly alarmed.

When I reached my room I wished to get to work at once, and read through the letters by daylight, since I do not see well by candle-light; but the wretched Mawra had got the idea of sweeping the floor. These blockheads of Finnish women are always clean where there is no need to be.

I then went for a little walk and began to think over what had happened. Now at last I could get to the bottom of all facts, ideas and motives! These letters would explain everything. Dogs are clever fellows; they know all about politics, and I will certainly find in the letters all I want, especially the character of the director and all his relationships. And through these letters I will get information about her who—but silence!

Towards evening I came home and lay for a good while on the bed.

November 13th.—Now let us see! The letter is fairly legible but the handwriting is somewhat doggish.

"Dear Fidel!—I cannot get accustomed to your ordinary name, as if they could not have found a better one for you! Fidel! How tasteless! How ordinary! But this is not the time to discuss it. I am very glad that we thought of corresponding with each other."

(The letter is quite correctly written. The punctuation and spelling are perfectly right. Even our head clerk does not write so simply and clearly, though he declares he has been at the University. Let us go on.)

"I think that it is one of the most refined joys of this world to interchange thoughts, feelings, and impressions."

(H'm! This idea comes from some book which has been translated from German. I can't remember the title.)

"I speak from experience, although I have not gone farther into the world than just before our front door. Does not my life pass happily and comfortably? My mistress, whom her father calls Sophie, is quite in love with me."

(Ah! Ah!—but better be silent!)

"Her father also often strokes me. I drink tea and coffee with cream. Yes, my dear, I must confess to you that I find no satisfaction in those large, gnawed-at bones which Polkan devours in the kitchen. Only the bones of wild fowl are good, and that only when the marrow has not been sucked out of them. They taste very nice with a little sauce, but there should be no green stuff in it. But I know nothing worse than the habit of giving dogs balls of bread kneaded up. Someone sits at table, kneads a bread-ball with dirty fingers, calls you and sticks it in your mouth. Good manners forbid your refusing it, and you eat it—with disgust it is true, but you eat it."

(The deuce! What is this? What rubbish! As if she could find nothing more suitable to write about! I will see if there is anything more reasonable on the second page.)

"I am quite willing to inform you of everything that goes on here. I have already mentioned the most important person in the house, whom Sophie calls 'Papa.' He is a very strange man."

(Ah! Here we are at last! Yes, I knew it; they have a politician's penetrating eye for all things. Let us see what she says about "Papa.")

"... a strange man. Generally he is silent; he only speaks seldom, but about a week ago he kept on repeating to himself, 'Shall I get it or not?' In one hand he took a sheet of paper; the other he stretched out as though to receive something, and repeated, 'Shall I get it or not?' Once he turned to me with the question, 'What do you think, Meggy?' I did not understand in the least what he meant, sniffed at his boots, and went away. A week later he came home with his face beaming. That morning he was visited by several officers in uniform who congratulated him. At the dinner-table he was in a better humour than I have ever seen him before."

(Ah! he is ambitious then! I must make a note of that.)

"Pardon, my dear, I hasten to conclude, etc., etc. To-morrow I will finish the letter."

. . . . . .

"Now, good morning; here I am again at your service. To-day my mistress Sophie ..."

(Ah! we will see what she says about Sophie. Let us go on!)

"... was in an unusually excited state. She went to a ball, and I was glad that I could write to you in her absence. She likes going to balls, although she gets dreadfully irritated while dressing. I cannot understand, my dear, what is the pleasure in going to a ball. She comes home from the ball at six o'clock in the early morning, and to judge by her pale and emaciated face, she has had nothing to eat. I could, frankly speaking, not endure such an existence. If I could not get partridge with sauce, or the wing of a roast chicken, I don't know what I should do. Porridge with sauce is also tolerable, but I can get up no enthusiasm for carrots, turnips, and artichokes."

The style is very unequal! One sees at once that it has not been written by a man. The beginning is quite intelligent, but at the end the canine nature breaks out. I will read another letter; it is rather long and there is no date.

"Ah, my dear, how delightful is the arrival of spring! My heart beats as though it expected something. There is a perpetual ringing in my ears, so that I often stand with my foot raised, for several minutes at a time, and listen towards the door. In confidence I will tell you that I have many admirers. I often sit on the window-sill and let them pass in review. Ah! if you knew what miscreations there are among them; one, a clumsy house-dog, with stupidity written on his face, walks the street with an important air and imagines that he is an extremely important person, and that the eyes of all the world are fastened on him. I don't pay him the least attention, and pretend not to see him at all.

"And what a hideous bulldog has taken up his post opposite my window! If he stood on his hind-legs, as the monster probably cannot, he would be taller by a head than my mistress's papa, who himself has a stately figure. This lout seems, moreover, to be very impudent. I growl at him, but he does not seem to mind that at all. If he at least would only wrinkle his forehead! Instead of that, he stretches out his tongue, droops his big ears, and stares in at the window— this rustic boor! But do you think, my dear, that my heart remains proof against all temptations? Alas no! If you had only seen that gentlemanly dog who crept through the fence of the neighbouring house. 'Treasure' is his name. Ah, my dear, what a delightful snout he has!"

(To the deuce with the stuff! What rubbish it is! How can one blacken paper with such absurdities. Give me a man. I want to see a man! I need some food to nourish and refresh my mind, and get this silliness instead. I will turn the page to see if there is anything better on the other side.)

"Sophie sat at the table and sewed something. I looked out of the window and amused myself by watching the passers-by. Suddenly a flunkey entered and announced a visitor—'Mr Teploff.'

"'Show him in!' said Sophie, and began to embrace me. 'Ah! Meggy, Meggy, do you know who that is? He is dark, and belongs to the Royal Household; and what eyes he has! Dark and brilliant as fire.'

"Sophie hastened into her room. A minute later a young gentleman with black whiskers entered. He went to the mirror, smoothed his hair, and looked round the room. I turned away and sat down in my place.

"Sophie entered and returned his bow in a friendly manner.

"I pretended to observe nothing, and continued to look out of the window. But I leant my head a little on one side to hear what they were talking about. Ah, my dear! what silly things they discussed—how a lady executed the wrong figure in dancing; how a certain Boboff, with his expansive shirt-frill, had looked like a stork and nearly fallen down; how a certain Lidina imagined she had blue eyes when they were really green, etc.

"I do not know, my dear, what special charm she finds in her Mr Teploff, and why she is so delighted with him."

(It seems to me myself that there is something wrong here. It is impossible that this Teploff should bewitch her. We will see further.)

"If this gentleman of the Household pleases her, then she must also be pleased, according to my view, with that official who sits in her papa's writing-room. Ah, my dear, if you know what a figure he is! A regular tortoise!"

(What official does she mean?)

"He has an extraordinary name. He always sits there and mends the pens. His hair looks like a truss of hay. Her papa always employs him instead of a servant."

(I believe this abominable little beast is referring to me. But what has my hair got to do with hay?)

"Sophie can never keep from laughing when she sees him."

You lie, cursed dog! What a scandalous tongue! As if I did not know that it is envy which prompts you, and that here there is treachery at work—yes, the treachery of the chief clerk. This man hates me implacably; he has plotted against me, he is always seeking to injure me. I'll look through one more letter; perhaps it will make the matter clearer.

"Fidel, my dear, pardon me that I have not written for so long. I was floating in a dream of delight. In truth, some author remarks, 'Love is a second life.' Besides, great changes are going on in the house. The young chamberlain is always here. Sophie is wildly in love with him. Her papa is quite contented. I heard from Gregor, who sweeps the floor, and is in the habit of talking to himself, that the marriage will soon be celebrated. Her papa will at any rate get his daughter married to a general, a colonel, or a chamberlain."

Deuce take it! I can read no more. It is all about chamberlains and generals. I should like myself to be a general—not in order to sue for her hand and all that—no, not at all; I should like to be a general merely in order to see people wriggling, squirming, and hatching plots before me.

And then I should like to tell them that they are both of them not worth spitting on. But it is vexatious! I tear the foolish dog's letters up in a thousand pieces.

December 3rd.—It is not possible that the marriage should take place; it is only idle gossip. What does it signify if he is a chamberlain! That is only a dignity, not a substantial thing which one can see or handle. His chamberlain's office will not procure him a third eye in his forehead. Neither is his nose made of gold; it is just like mine or anyone else's nose. He does not eat and cough, but smells and sneezes with it. I should like to get to the bottom of the mystery—whence do all these distinctions come? Why am I only a titular councillor?

Perhaps I am really a count or a general, and only appear to be a titular councillor. Perhaps I don't even know who and what I am. How many cases there are in history of a simple gentleman, or even a burgher or peasant, suddenly turning out to be a great lord or baron? Well, suppose that I appear suddenly in a general's uniform, on the right shoulder an epaulette, on the left an epaulette, and a blue sash across my breast, what sort of a tune would my beloved sing then? What would her papa, our director, say? Oh, he is ambitious! He is a freemason, certainly a freemason; however much he may conceal it, I have found it out. When he gives anyone his hand, he only reaches out two fingers. Well, could not I this minute be nominated a general or a superintendent? I should like to know why I am a titular councillor—why just that, and nothing more?

December 5th.—To-day I have been reading papers the whole morning. Very strange things are happening in Spain. I have not understood them all. It is said that the throne is vacant, the representatives of the people are in difficulties about finding an occupant, and riots are taking place.

All this appears to me very strange. How can the throne be vacant? It is said that it will be occupied by a woman. A woman cannot sit on a throne. That is impossible. Only a king can sit on a throne. They say that there is no king there, but that is not possible. There cannot be a kingdom without a king. There must be a king, but he is hidden away somewhere. Perhaps he is actually on the spot, and only some domestic complications, or fears of the neighbouring Powers, France and other countries, compel him to remain in concealment; there might also be other reasons.

116

December 8th.—I was nearly going to the office, but various considerations kept me from doing so. I keep on thinking about these Spanish affairs. How is it possible that a woman should reign? It would not be allowed, especially by England. In the rest of Europe the political situation is also critical; the Emperor of Austria——

These events, to tell the truth, have so shaken and shattered me, that I could really do nothing all day. Mawra told me that I was very absent-minded at table. In fact, in my absent-mindedness I threw two plates on the ground so that they broke in pieces.

After dinner I felt weak, and did not feel up to making abstracts of reports. I lay most of the time on my bed, and thought of the Spanish affairs.

The year 2000: April 43rd.—To-day is a day of splendid triumph. Spain has a king; he has been found, and I am he. I discovered it to-day; all of a sudden it came upon me like a flash of lightning.

I do not understand how I could imagine that I am a titular councillor. How could such a foolish idea enter my head? It was fortunate that it occurred to no one to shut me up in an asylum. Now it is all clear, and as plain as a pikestaff. Formerly—I don't know why—everything seemed veiled in a kind of mist. That is, I believe, because people think that the human brain is in the head. Nothing of the sort; it is carried by the wind from the Caspian Sea.

For the first time I told Mawra who I am. When she learned that the king of Spain stood before her, she struck her hands together over her head, and nearly died of alarm. The stupid thing had never seen the king of Spain before!

I comforted her, however, at once by assuring her that I was not angry with her for having hitherto cleaned my boots badly. Women are stupid things; one cannot interest them in lofty subjects. She was frightened because she thought all kings of Spain were like Philip II. But I explained to her that there was a great difference between me and him. I did not go to the office. Why the deuce should I? No, my dear friends, you won't get me there again! I am not going to worry myself with your infernal documents any more.

Marchember 86. Between day and night.—To-day the office-messenger came and summoned me, as I had not been there for three weeks. I went just for the fun of the thing. The chief clerk thought I would bow humbly before him, and make excuses; but I looked at him quite indifferently, neither angrily nor mildly, and sat down quietly at my place as though I noticed no one. I looked at all this rabble of scribblers, and thought, "If you only knew who is sitting among you! Good heavens! what a to-do you would make. Even the chief clerk would bow himself to the earth before me as he does now before the director."

A pile of reports was laid before me, of which to make abstracts, but I did not touch them with one finger.

After a little time there was a commotion in the office, and there a report went round that the director was coming. Many of the clerks vied with each other to attract his notice; but I did not stir. As he came through our room, each one hastily buttoned up his coat; but I had no idea of doing anything of the sort. What is the director to me? Should I stand up before him? Never. What sort of a director is he? He is a bottle-stopper, and no director. A quite ordinary, simple bottle-stopper—nothing more. I felt quite amused as they gave me a document to sign.

They thought I would simply put down my name— "So-and-so, Clerk." Why not? But at the top of the sheet, where the director generally writes his name, I inscribed "Ferdinand VIII." in bold characters. You should have seen what a reverential silence ensued. But I made a gesture with my hand, and said, "Gentlemen, no ceremony please!" Then I went out, and took my way straight to the director's house.

He was not at home. The flunkey wanted not to let me in, but I talked to him in such a way that he soon dropped his arms.

I went straight to Sophie's dressing-room. She sat before the mirror. When she saw me, she sprang up and took a step backwards; but I did not tell her that I was the king of Spain.

But I told her that a happiness awaited her, beyond her power to imagine; and that in spite of all our enemies' devices we should be united. That was all which I wished to say to her, and I went out. Oh, what cunning creatures these women are! Now I have found out what woman really is. Hitherto no one knew whom a woman really loves; I am the first to discover it—she loves the devil. Yes, joking apart, learned men write nonsense when they pronounce that she is this and that; she loves the devil—that is all. You see a woman looking through her lorgnette from a box in the front row. One thinks she is watching that stout gentleman who wears an order. Not a bit of it! She is watching the devil who stands behind his back. He has hidden himself there, and beckons to her with his finger. And she marries him—actually—she marries him!

That is all ambition, and the reason is that there is under the tongue a little blister in which there is a little worm of the size of a pin's head. And this is constructed by a barber in Bean Street; I don't remember his name at the moment, but so much is certain that, in conjunction with a midwife, he wants to spread Mohammedanism all over the world, and that in consequence of this a large number of people in France have already adopted the faith of Islam.

No date. The day had no date.—I went for a walk incognito on the Nevski Prospect. I avoided every appearance of being the king of Spain. I felt it below my dignity to let myself be recognised by the whole world, since I must first present myself at court. And I was also restrained by the fact that I have at present no Spanish national costume. If I could only get a cloak! I tried to have a consultation with a tailor, but these people are real asses! Moreover, they neglect their business, dabble in speculation, and have become loafers. I will have a cloak made out of my new official uniform which I have only worn twice. But to prevent this botcher of a tailor spoiling it, I will make it myself with closed doors, so that no one sees me. Since the cut must be altogether altered, I have used the scissors myself.

I don't remember the date. The devil knows what month it was. The cloak is quite ready. Mawra exclaimed aloud when I put it on. I will, however, not present myself at court yet; the Spanish deputation has not yet arrived. It would not be befitting if I appeared without them. My appearance would be less imposing. From hour to hour I expect them.

The 1st.—The extraordinary long delay of the deputies in coming astonishes me. What can possibly keep them? Perhaps France has a hand in the matter; it is certainly hostilely inclined. I went to the post office to inquire whether the Spanish deputation had come. The postmaster is an extraordinary blockhead who knows nothing. "No," he said to me, "there is no Spanish deputation here; but if you want to send them a letter, we will forward it at the fixed rate." The deuce! What do I want with a letter? Letters are nonsense. Letters are written by apothecaries....

Madrid, February 30th.—So I am in Spain after all! It has happened so quickly that I could hardly take it in. The Spanish deputies came early this morning, and I got with them into the carriage. This unexpected promptness seemed to me strange. We drove so quickly that in half an hour we were at the Spanish frontier. Over all Europe now there are cast-iron roads, and the steamers go very fast. A wonderful country, this Spain!

As we entered the first room, I saw numerous persons with shorn heads. I guessed at once that they must be either grandees or soldiers, at least to judge by their shorn heads.

The Chancellor of the State, who led me by the hand, seemed to me to behave in a very strange way; he pushed me into a little room and said, "Stay here, and if you call yourself 'King Ferdinand' again, I will drive the wish to do so out of you."

I knew, however, that that was only a test, and I reasserted my conviction; on which the Chancellor gave me two such severe blows with a stick on the back, that I could have cried out with the pain. But I restrained myself, remembering that this was a usual ceremony of old-time chivalry when one was inducted into a high position, and in Spain the laws of chivalry prevail up to the present day. When I was alone, I determined to study State affairs; I discovered that Spain and

China are one and the same country, and it is only through ignorance that people regard them as separate kingdoms. I advise everyone urgently to write down the word "Spain" on a sheet of paper; he will see that it is quite the same as China.

But I feel much annoyed by an event which is about to take place to-morrow; at seven o'clock the earth is going to sit on the moon. This is foretold by the famous English chemist, Wellington. To tell the truth, I often felt uneasy when I thought of the excessive brittleness and fragility of the moon. The moon is generally repaired in Hamburg, and very imperfectly. It is done by a lame cooper, an obvious blockhead who has no idea how to do it. He took waxed thread and olive-oil—hence that pungent smell over all the earth which compels people to hold their noses. And this makes the moon so fragile that no men can live on it, but only noses. Therefore we cannot see our noses, because they are on the moon.

When I now pictured to myself how the earth, that massive body, would crush our noses to dust, if it sat on the moon, I became so uneasy, that I immediately put on my shoes and stockings and hastened into the council-hall to give the police orders to prevent the earth sitting on the moon.

The grandees with the shorn heads, whom I met in great numbers in the hall, were very intelligent people, and when I exclaimed, "Gentlemen! let us save the moon, for the earth is going to sit on it," they all set to work to fulfil my imperial wish, and many of them clambered up the wall in order to take the moon down. At that moment the Imperial Chancellor came in. As soon as he appeared, they all scattered, but I alone, as king, remained. To my astonishment, however, the Chancellor beat me with the stick and drove me to my room. So powerful are ancient customs in Spain!

January in the same year, following after February.—I can never understand what kind of a country this Spain really is. The popular customs and rules of court etiquette are quite extraordinary. I do not understand them at all, at all. To-day my head was shorn, although I exclaimed as loudly as I could, that I did not want to be a monk. What happened afterwards, when they began to let cold water trickle on my head, I do not know. I have never experienced such hellish torments. I nearly went mad, and they had difficulty in holding me. The significance of this strange custom is entirely hidden from me. It is a very foolish and unreasonable one.

Nor can I understand the stupidity of the kings who have not done away with it before now. Judging by all the circumstances, it seems to me as though I had fallen into the hands of the Inquisition, and as though the man whom I took to be the Chancellor was the Grand Inquisitor. But yet I cannot understand how the king could fall into the hands of the Inquisition. The affair may have been arranged by France—especially Polignac—he is a hound, that Polignac! He has sworn to compass my death, and now he is hunting me down. But I know, my friend, that you are only a tool of the English. They are clever fellows, and have a finger in every pie. All the world knows that France sneezes when England takes a pinch of snuff.

The 25th.—To-day the Grand Inquisitor came into my room; when I heard his steps in the distance, I hid myself under a chair. When he did not see me, he began to call. At first he called "Poprishchin!" I made no answer. Then he called "Axanti Ivanovitch! Titular Councillor! Nobleman!" I still kept silence. "Ferdinand the Eighth, King of Spain!" I was on the point of putting out my head, but I thought, "No, brother, you shall not deceive me! You shall not pour water on my head again!"

But he had already seen me and drove me from under the chair with his stick. The cursed stick really hurts one. But the following discovery compensated me for all the pain, i.e. that every cock has his Spain under his feathers. The Grand Inquisitor went angrily away, and threatened me with some punishment or other. I felt only contempt for his powerless spite, for I know that he only works like a machine, like a tool of the English.

34 March. February, 349.—No, I have no longer power to endure. O God! what are they going to do with me? They pour cold water on my head. They take no notice of me, and seem neither to see nor hear. Why do they torture me? What do they want from one so wretched as myself? What can I give them? I possess nothing. I cannot bear all their tortures; my head aches as though everything were turning round in a circle. Save me! Carry me away! Give me three steeds swift as the wind! Mount your seat, coachman, ring bells, gallop horses, and carry me straight out of this world. Farther, ever farther, till nothing more is to be seen!

Ah! the heaven bends over me already; a star glimmers in the distance; the forest with its dark trees in the moonlight rushes past; a bluish mist floats under my feet; music sounds in the cloud; on the one side is the sea, on the other, Italy; beyond I also see Russian peasants' houses. Is not my parents' house there in the distance? Does not my mother sit by the window? O mother, mother, save your unhappy son! Let a tear fall on his aching head! See how they torture him! Press the poor orphan to your bosom! He has no rest in this world; they hunt him from place to place.

Mother, mother, have pity on your sick child! And do you know that the Bey of Algiers has a wart under his nose?

A MAY NIGHT

I

Songs were echoing in the village street. It was just the time when the young men and girls, tired with the work and cares of the day, were in the habit of assembling for the dance. In the mild evening light, cheerful songs blended with mild melodies. A mysterious twilight obscured the blue sky and made everything seem indistinct and distant. It was growing dark, but the songs were not hushed.

A young Cossack, Levko by name, the son of the village headman, had stolen away from the singers, guitar in hand. With his embroidered cap set awry on his head, and his hand playing over the strings, he stepped a measure to the music. Then he stopped at the door of a house half hidden by blossoming cherry-trees. Whose house was it? To whom did the door lead? After a little while he played and sang:

"The night is nigh, the sun is down,

Come out to me, my love, my own!"

"No one is there; my bright-eyed beauty is fast asleep," said the Cossack to himself as he finished the song and approached the window. "Hanna, Hanna, are you asleep, or won't you come to me? Perhaps you are afraid someone

127

will see us, or will not expose your delicate face to the cold! Fear nothing! The evening is warm, and there is no one near. And if anyone comes I will wrap you in my caftan, fold you in my arms, and no one will see us. And if the wind blows cold, I will press you close to my heart, warm you with my kisses, and lay my cap on your tiny feet, my darling. Only throw me a single glance. No, you are not asleep, you proud thing!" he exclaimed now louder, in a voice which betrayed his annoyance at the humiliation. "You are laughing at me! Good-bye!"

Then he turned away, set his cap jauntily, and, still lightly touching his guitar, stepped back from the window. Just then the wooden handle of the door turned with a grating noise, and a girl who counted hardly seventeen springs looked out timidly through the darkness, and still keeping hold of the handle, stepped over the threshold. In the twilight her bright eyes shone like little stars, her coral necklace gleamed, and the pink flush on her cheeks did not escape the Cossack's observation.

"How impatient you are!" she said in a whisper. "You get angry so quickly! Why did you choose such a time? There are crowds of people in the street.... I tremble all over."

"Don't tremble, my darling! Come close to me!" said the Cossack, putting down his guitar, which hung on a long strap round his neck, and sitting down with her on the doorstep. "You know I find it hard to be only an hour without seeing you."

"Do you know what I am thinking of?" interrupted the young girl, looking at him thoughtfully. "Something whispers to me that we shall not see so much of each other in the future. The people here are not well disposed to you, the girls look so envious, and the young fellows.... I notice also that my mother watches me carefully for some time past. I must confess I was happier when among strangers." Her face wore a troubled expression as she spoke.

"You are only two months back at home, and are already tired of it!" said the Cossack. "And of me too perhaps?"

"Oh no!" she replied, smiling. "I love you, you black-eyed Cossack! I love you because of your dark eyes, and my heart laughs in my breast when you look at me. I feel so happy when you come down the street stroking your black moustache, and enjoy listening to your song when you play the guitar!"

"Oh my Hanna!" exclaimed the Cossack, kissing the girl and drawing her closer to him.

"Stop, Levko! Tell me whether you have spoken to your father?"

"About what?" he answered absent-mindedly. "About my marrying you? Yes, I did." But he seemed to speak almost reluctantly.

"Well? What more?"

"What can you make of him? The old curmudgeon pretends to be deaf; he will not listen to anything, and blames me for loafing with fellows, as he says, about the streets. But don't worry, Hanna! I give you my word as a Cossack, I will break his obstinacy."

"You only need to say a word, Levko, and it shall be as you wish. I know that of myself. Often I do not wish to obey you, but you speak only a word, and I involuntarily do what you wish. Look, look!" she continued, laying her head on his shoulder and raising her eyes to the sky, the immeasurable heaven of the Ukraine; "there far away are twinkling little stars—one, two, three, four, five. Is it not true that those are angels opening the windows of their bright little homes and looking down on us. Is it not so, Levko? They are looking down on earth. If men had wings like birds, how high they could fly. But ah! not even our oaks reach the sky. Still people say there is in some distant land a tree whose top reaches to heaven, and that God descends by it on the earth, the night before Easter."

"No, Hanna. God has a long ladder which reaches from heaven to earth. Before Easter Sunday holy angels set it up, and as soon as God puts His foot on the first rung, all evil spirits take to flight and fall in swarms into hell. That is why on Easter Day there are none of them on earth."

"How gently the water ripples! Like a child in the cradle," continued Hanna, pointing to the pool begirt by dark maples and weeping-willows, whose melancholy branches drooped in the water. On a hill near the wood slumbered an old house with closed shutters. The roof was covered with moss and weeds; leafy apple-trees had grown high up before the windows; the wood cast deep shadows on it; a grove of nut-trees spread from the foot of the hill as far as the pool.

"I remember as if in a dream," said Hanna, keeping her eyes fixed on the house, "a long, long time ago, when I was little and lived with mother, someone told a terrible story about this house. You must know it—tell me."

"God forbid, my dear child! Old women and stupid people talk a lot of nonsense. It would only frighten you and spoil your sleep."

"Tell me, my darling, my black-eyed Cossack," she said, pressing her cheek to his. "No, you don't love me; you have certainly another sweetheart! I will not be frightened, and will sleep quite quietly. If you refuse to tell me, *that* would keep me awake. I would keep on worrying and thinking about it. Tell me, Levko!"

"Certainly it is true what people say, that the devil possesses girls, and stirs up their curiosity. Well then, listen. Long ago there lived in that house an elderly man who had a beautiful daughter white as snow, just like you. His wife had been dead a long time, and he was thinking of marrying again.

"'Will you pet me as before, father, if you take a second wife?' asked his daughter.

"'Yes, my daughter,' he answered, 'I shall love you more than ever, and give you yet more rings and necklaces.'

"So he brought a young wife home, who was beautiful and white and red, but she cast such an evil glance at her stepdaughter that she cried aloud, but not a word did her sulky stepmother speak to her all day long.

"When night came, and her father and his wife had retired, the young girl locked herself up in her room, and feeling melancholy began to weep bitterly. Suddenly she spied a hideous black cat creeping towards her; its fur was aflame and its claws struck on the ground like iron. In her terror the girl sprang on a chair; the cat followed her. Then she sprang into bed; the cat sprang after her, and seizing her by the throat began to choke her. She tore the creature away, and flung it on the ground, but the terrible cat began to creep towards her again. Rendered desperate with terror, she seized her father's sabre which hung on the wall, and struck at the cat, wounding one of its paws. The animal disappeared, whimpering.

"The next day the young wife did not leave her bedroom; the third day she appeared with her hand bound up.

"The poor girl perceived that her stepmother was a witch, and that she had wounded her hand.

"On the fourth day her father told her to bring water, to sweep the floor like a servant-maid, and not to show herself where he and his wife sat. She obeyed him, though with a heavy heart. On the fifth day he drove her barefooted out of the house, without giving her any food for her journey. Then she began to sob and covered her face with her hands.

"'You have ruined your own daughter, father!' she cried; 'and the witch has ruined your soul. May God forgive you! He will not allow me to live much longer.'

"And do you see," continued Levko, turning to Hanna and pointing to the house, "do you see that high bank; from that bank she threw herself into the water, and has been no more seen on earth."

"And the witch?" Hanna interrupted, timidly fastening her tearful eyes on him.

"The witch? Old women say that when the moon shines, all those who have been drowned come out to warm themselves in its rays, and that they are led by the witch's stepdaughter. One night she saw her stepmother by the pool, caught hold of her, and dragged her screaming into the water. But this time also the witch played her a trick; she changed herself into one of those who had been drowned, and so escaped the chastisement she would have received at their hands.

"Let anyone who likes believe the old women's stories. They say that the witch's stepdaughter gathers together those who have been drowned every night, and looks in their faces in order to find out which of them is the witch; but has not done so yet. Such are the old wives' tales. It is said to be the intention of the present owner to erect a distillery on the spot. But I hear voices. They are coming home from the dancing. Good-bye, Hanna! Sleep well, and don't think of all that nonsense." So saying he embraced her, kissed her, and departed.

"Good-bye, Levko!" said Hanna, still gazing at the dark pine wood.

The brilliant moon was now rising and filling all the earth with splendour. The pool shone like silver, and the shadows of the trees stood out in strong relief.

"Good-bye, Hanna!" she heard again as she spoke, and felt the light pressure of a kiss.

"You have come back!" she said, looking round, but started on seeing a stranger before her.

There was another "Good-bye, Hanna!" and again she was kissed.

"Has the devil brought a second?" she exclaimed angrily.

"Good-bye, dear Hanna!"

"There is a third!"

"Good-bye, good-bye, good-bye, Hanna!" and kisses rained from all sides.

"Why, there is a whole band of them!" cried Hanna, tearing herself from the youths who had gathered round. "Are they never tired of the eternal kissing? I shall soon not be able to show myself on the street!" So saying, she closed the door and bolted it.

II
THE VILLAGE HEADMAN

Do you know a Ukraine night? No, you do not know a night in the Ukraine. Gaze your full on it. The moon shines in the midst of the sky; the immeasurable vault of heaven seems to have expanded to infinity; the earth is bathed in silver light; the air is warm, voluptuous, and redolent of innumerable sweet scents. Divine night! Magical night! Motionless, but inspired with divine breath, the forests stand, casting enormous shadows and wrapped in complete darkness. Calmly and placidly sleep the lakes surrounded by dark green thickets. The virginal groves of the hawthorns and cherry-trees stretch their roots timidly into the cool water; only now and then their leaves rustle unwillingly when that freebooter, the night-wind, steals up to kiss them. The whole landscape is hushed in slumber; but there is a mysterious breath upon the heights. One falls into a weird and unearthly mood, and silvery apparitions rise from the depths. Divine night! Magical night! Suddenly the woods, lakes, and steppes become alive. The nightingales of the Ukraine are singing, and it seems as though the moon itself were listening to their song. The village sleeps as though under a magic spell; the cottages shine in the moonlight against the darkness of the woods behind them. The songs grow silent, and all is still. Only here and there is a glimmer of light in some small window. Some families, sitting up late, are finishing their supper at the thresholds of their houses.

"No, the 'gallop' is not danced like that! Now I see, it does not go properly! What did my godfather tell me? So then! Hop! tralala! Hop! tralala! Hop! Hop! Hop!" Thus a half-intoxicated, middle-aged Cossack talked to himself as he danced through the street. "By heaven, a 'gallop' is not danced like that! What is the use of lying! On with it then! Hop! tralala! Hop! tralala! Hop! Hop! Hop!"

"See that fool there! If he were only a young fellow! But to see a grown man dancing, and the children laughing at him," exclaimed an old woman who was passing by, carrying a bundle of straw. "Go home! It is quite time to go to sleep!"

"I am going!" said the Cossack, standing still. "I am going. What do I care about the headman? He thinks because he is the eldest, and throws cold water on people, and carries his head high. As to being headman—I myself am a headman. Yes indeed—otherwise——" As he spoke, he stepped up to the door of the first cottage he came to, stood at the window, drumming with his fingers on the glass, and feeling for the door-handle. "Woman, open! Woman, open quickly I tell you! It is time for me to go to sleep!"

"Where are you going, Kalenik? That is the wrong house!" some young girls who were returning from the dance called to him as they passed. "Shall we show you yours?"

"Yes, please, ladies!"

"Ladies! Just listen to him!" one of them exclaimed. "How polite Kalenik is! We will show you the house—but no, first dance before us!"

"Dance before you? Oh, you are clever girls!" said Kalenik in a drawling voice, and laughing. He threatened them with his finger, and stumbled, not being able to stand steadily. "And will you let yourselves be kissed? I will kiss the lot." With tottering steps he began to run after them.

The girls cried out and ran apart; but they soon plucked up courage and went on the other side of the road, when they saw that Kalenik was not firm on his legs.

"There is your house!" they called to him, pointing to one which was larger than the rest, and which belonged to the village headman.

Kalenik turned towards it, and began again to revile the headman.

But who is this headman to whose disadvantage so much has been said? Oh, he is a very important person in the village. Before Kalenik reaches his house, we shall doubtless find enough time to say something about him. Everyone in the village takes off his cap at the sight of him, and even the smallest girls wish him good morning. Which of the young Cossacks would not like to be a headman? The headman has an entry everywhere, and every stalwart rustic stands respectfully, cap in hand, so long as the headman feels round his snuff-box with his thick, coarse finger. In parish-meetings and other assemblies, although his power may be limited by the votes of the majority, the headman still maintains the upper hand, and sends whom he chooses to make roads or dig ditches. In outward manners he is morose and severe, and not fond of talking. Long ago, when the Empress Catherine of blessed memory journeyed to the Crimea, he was chosen as one of her escort for two whole days, and had the high honour of sitting with the imperial coachman on the box.

Since then the headman has formed the habit of shaking his head solemnly and thoughtfully, of stroking his long, drooping moustache, and of darting hawk-like glances from his eyes. Whatever the topic of conversation may be, he manages to refer to his having accompanied the Empress, and sat on the box of the imperial coach. He often pretends to be hard of hearing, especially when he hears something that he does not like. He has an aversion for dandies, and himself wears under a black caftan of cloth, made at home, a simple, embroidered, woollen waist-band. No one has seen him wear any other dress except, of course, on the occasion of the Czarina's journey to the Crimea, when he wore a blue Cossack's uniform. Hardly anyone in the village remembers that time, and he keeps the uniform packed up in a chest.

The headman is a widower, but his sister-in-law lives with him. She cooks his dinner and supper, keeps the house and furniture clean, weaves linen, and acts as housekeeper generally. The village gossips say that she is not a relation of his; but we must remark that the headman has many enemies who spread all kinds of slanders about him. We have now said what we considered to be necessary about the headman, and the drunken Kalenik is not yet half-way to his house. He continued to abuse the headman in terms which might be expected from one in his condition.

III
AN UNEXPECTED RIVAL—THE CONSPIRACY

"No, you fellows, I won't. What is the good of all those silly goings-on? Aren't you tired of these foolish jokes? People already call us good-for-nothing scapegraces. Better go to bed!" So Levko said one evening to his companions, who were trying to persuade him to take part with them in further practical jokes. "Farewell, brothers! Good night!" he said, and left them with quick steps.

"Does my bright-eyed Hanna sleep?" he thought as he passed the house shaded by the cherry-trees. Then in the silence he heard the sound of a whispered conversation. Levko stood still. Between the trees there glimmered something white. "What is that?" he thought, as he crept closer and hid himself behind a tree.

By the light of the moon he saw the face of a girl standing opposite him. It was Hanna. But who was the tall man who had his back turned to him? In vain he strained his eyes; the whole figure was hidden in shadow, and the slightest forward step on Levko's part would expose him to the risk of discovery. He therefore leant quietly against the tree, and determined to remain where he was. Then he heard the girl utter his name distinctly.

"Levko? Levko is a baby," said the tall man in an undertone. "If I ever find him with you, I will pull his hair."

"I should like to know what rascal is boasting of pulling my hair," said Levko to himself, stretching out his head and endeavouring to miss no word. But the stranger continued to speak so low that he was inaudible.

"What, aren't you ashamed?" said Hanna after he had finished. "You are lying and deceiving me; I will never believe that you love me."

"I know," continued the tall man, "that Levko has talked nonsense to you and turned your head." (Here it seemed to the Cossack as though the stranger's voice were not quite unknown to him, and that he must have heard it somewhere or other.) "But Levko shall learn to know me," continued the stranger. "He thinks I don't notice his rascally tricks; but he will yet feel the weight of my fists, the scoundrel!"

At these words Levko could no longer restrain his wrath. He came three steps nearer, and took a run in order to plant a blow which would have stretched the stranger on the ground in spite of his strength. At that moment, however, a ray of light fell on the latter's face, and Levko stood transfixed, for he saw it was his father. But he only expressed his surprise by an involuntary shake of the head and a low whistle.

On the other side there was the sound of approaching footsteps. Hanna ran hastily into the house and closed the door behind her.

"Good-bye, Hanna!" cried one of the youths, who had stolen up and embraced the headman, but started back alarmed when he felt a rough moustache.

"Good-bye, my darling!" cried another, but speedily executed a somersault in consequence of a violent blow from the headman.

"Good-bye, good-bye, Hanna!" exclaimed several youths, falling on his neck.

141

"Go to the deuce, you infernal scoundrels!" shouted the headman, defending himself with both hands and feet. "What kind of Hanna do you take me for? Hang yourselves like your fathers did, you children of the devil! Falling on one like flies on honey! I will show you who Hanna is!"

"The headman! The headman! It is the headman!" cried the youths, running away in all directions.

"Aha, father!" said Levko to himself, recovering from his astonishment and looking after the headman as he departed, cursing and scolding. "Those are the tricks you like to play! Splendid! And I wonder and puzzle my head why he pretends to be deaf when I only touch on the matter! Wait, you old sinner, I will teach you to cajole other people's sweethearts. Hi! you fellows, come here!" he cried, beckoning to the youths, who gathered round him. "Come nearer! I told you to go to bed, but I am differently minded now, and am ready to go round with you all night."

"That is reasonable," exclaimed a broad-shouldered, stout fellow, who was regarded as the chief toper and good-for-nothing in the village. "I always feel uncomfortable if I do not have a good fling, and play some practical jokes. I always feel as though there were something wanting, as though I had lost my cap or my pipe—in a word, I don't feel like a proper Cossack then!"

"Do you really want to bait the headman?" asked Levko.

"The headman?"

"Yes, the headman. I don't know for whom he takes himself. He carries on as though he were a duke. It is not only that he treats us as if we were his serfs, but he comes after our girls."

"Quite right! That is true!" exclaimed all the youths together.

"But are we made of any worse stuff than he? We are, thank God! free Cossacks. Let us show him so."

"Yes, we will show him!" they shouted. "But when we go for the headman, we must not forget his clerk."

"The clerk shall have his share, too. Just now a song that suits the headman occurs to me. Go on! I will teach it you!" continued Levko, striking the strings of his guitar. "But listen! Disguise yourselves as well as you can."

"Hurrah for the Cossacks!" cried the stout reveller, dancing and clapping his hands. "Long live freedom! When one lets the reins go, one thinks of the good old times. It feels as jolly as though one were in paradise. Hurrah, you fellows! Go ahead!"

The youths rushed noisily through the village street, and the pious old women, aroused from their sleep, looked through the windows, crossed themselves drowsily, and thought, "There they go, the wild young fellows!"

IV
WILD PRANKS

Only in one house at the end of the street there still burned a light; it was the headman's. He had long finished his supper, and would certainly have gone to sleep but that he had a guest with him, the brandy-distiller. The latter had been sent to superintend the building of a distillery for the lords of the manor, who possessed small allotments between the lands of the free Cossacks. At the upper end of the table, in the place of honour, sat the guest—a short, stout man with small, merry eyes. He smoked his short pipe with obvious satisfaction, spitting every moment and constantly pushing the tobacco down in the bowl. The clouds of smoke collected over his head, and veiled him in a bluish mist. It seemed as though the broad chimney of a distillery, which was bored at always being perched up on the roof, had hit upon the idea of taking a little recreation, and had now settled itself comfortably at the headman's table. Close under his nose bristled his short, thick moustache, which in the dim, smoky atmosphere resembled a mouse which the distiller had caught and held in his mouth, usurping the functions of a dining-room cat. The headman sat there, as master of the house, wearing only his shirt and linen breeches. His eagle eye began to grow dim like the setting sun, and to half close. At the lower end of the table sat, smoking his pipe, one of the village council, of which the headman was superintendent. Out of respect for the latter he had not removed his caftan.

"How soon do you think," asked the headman, turning to the distiller and putting his hand before his gaping mouth, "will you have the distillery put up?"

"With God's help we shall be distilling brandy this autumn. On Conception Day I bet the headman will be tracing the figure eight with his feet on his way home." So saying, the distiller laughed so heartily that his small eyes disappeared altogether, his body was convulsed, and his twitching lips actually let go of the reeking pipe for a moment.

"God grant it!" said the headman, on whose face the shadow of a smile was visible. "Now, thank heaven, the number of distilleries is increasing a little; but in the old days, when I accompanied the Czarina on the Perejlaslov Road, and the late Besborodko――"

"Yes, my friend, those were bad times. Then from Krementchuk to Romen there were hardly two distilleries. And now—but have you heard what the infernal Germans have invented? They say they will no longer use wood for fuel in the distilleries, but devilish steam." At these words the distiller stared at the table reflectively, and at his arms resting on it. "But how they can use steam—by heavens! I don't know."

"What fools these Germans are!" said the headman. "I should like to give these sons of dogs a good thrashing. Whoever heard of cooking with steam? At this rate one will not be able to get a spoonful of porridge or a bit of bacon into one's mouth."

"And you, friend," broke in the headman's sister-in-law, who was sitting by the stove; "will you be with us the whole time without your wife?"

"Do I want her then? If she were only passably good-looking——"

"She is not pretty, then?" asked the headman with a questioning glance.

"How should she be; as old as Satan, and with a face as full of wrinkles as an empty purse," said the distiller, shaking again with laughter.

Then a noise was heard at the door, which opened and a Cossack stepped over the threshold without removing his cap, and remained standing in an absent-minded way in the middle of the room, with open mouth and gazing at the ceiling. It was Kalenik, whose acquaintance we have already made.

"Now I am at home," he said, taking his seat by the door, without taking any notice of those present. "Ah! to what a length Satan made the road stretch. I went on and on, and there was no end. My legs are quite broken. Woman, bring me my fur blanket to lie down on. There it is in the corner; but mind you don't upset the little pot of snuff. But no; better not touch it! Leave it alone! You are really quite drunk—I had better get it myself."

Kalenik tried to rise, but an invincible power fettered him to his seat.

"That's a nice business!" said the headman. "He comes into a strange house, and behaves as though he were at home! Push him out, in heaven's name!"

"Let him rest a bit, friend!" said the distiller, seizing the headman's arm. "The man is very useful; if we had only plenty of this kind, our distillery would get on grandly...." For the rest, it was not good-nature which inspired these words. The distiller was full of superstition, and to turn out a man who had already sat down, seemed to him to be tantamount to invoking the devil.

"That comes of being old," grumbled Kalenik, stretching himself out along the seat. "People might say I was drunk, but no, I am not! Why should I lie? I am ready to tell the headman to his face! Who is the headman anyway? May he break his neck, the son of a dog! I spit at him! May he be run over by a cart, the one-eyed devil!"

"Ah! the drunken sot has crawled into the house, and now he lays his paws on the table," said the headman, rising angrily; but at that moment a heavy stone, breaking a window-pane to pieces, fell at his feet. The headman remained standing. "If I knew," he said, "what jail-bird has thrown it, I would give him something. What devil's trick is this?" he continued, looking at the stone, which he held in his hand, with burning eyes. "I wish I could choke him with it!"

"Stop! Stop! God preserve you, friend!" broke in the distiller, looking pale. "God keep you in this world and the next, but don't curse anyone so."

"Ah! now we have his defender! May he be ruined!"

"Listen, friend! You don't know what happened to my late mother-in-law."

"Your mother-in-law?"

"Yes, my mother-in-law. One evening, perhaps rather earlier than this, they were sitting at supper, my late mother-in-law, my father-in-law, their two servants, and five children. My mother-in-law emptied some dumplings from the cooking-pot into a dish in order to cool them. But the others, being hungry after the day's work, did not wait till they were quite cooled, but stuck their long wooden forks into them and ate them at once. All at once a stranger entered—heaven knows whence!—and asked to be allowed to share their meal. They could not refuse to feed a hungry man, and gave him also a wooden fork. But the guest made as short work with the dumplings as a cow with hay. Before the family had each of them finished his or her dumpling and reached out their forks again for another, the dish had been swept as clean as the floor of a nobleman's drawing-room. My mother-in-law

148

emptied out some more dumplings; she thought to herself, 'Now the guest is satisfied, and will not be so greedy.' But on the contrary, he began to swallow them faster than ever, and emptied the second dish also. 'May one of them choke you!' said my mother-in-law under her breath. Suddenly the guest seemed to try to clear his throat, and fell back. They rushed to his help, but his breath had stopped and he was dead."

"Served him right, the cursed glutton!"

"But it turned out quite otherwise; since that time my mother-in-law has no rest. No sooner is it dark than the dead man approaches the house. He then sits astride the chimney, the scoundrel, holding a dumpling between his teeth. During the day it is quite quiet—one hears and sees nothing; but as soon as it begins to grow dark, and one casts a look at the roof, there he is comfortably perched on the chimney!"

"A wonderful story, friend! I heard something similar from my late——"

Then the headman suddenly stopped. Outside there were noises, and the stamping of dancers' feet. The strings of a guitar were being struck gently, to the accompaniment of a voice. Then the guitar was played more loudly, many voices joined in, and the whole chorus struck up a song in ridicule of the headman.

When it was over, the distiller said, with his head bent a little on one side, to the headman who was almost petrified by the audacity of the serenaders, "A fine song, my friend!"

"Very fine! Only it is a pity that they insult the headman."

He folded his arms with a certain measure of composure on the table, and prepared to listen further, for the singing and noise outside continued. A sharp observer, however, would have seen that it was not mere torpidity which made the headman sit so quietly. In the same way a crafty cat often allows an inexperienced mouse to play about her tail, while she is quickly devising a plan to cut it off from the mouse-hole. The headman's one eye was still fastened on the window, and his hand, after he had given the village councillor a sign, was reaching for the door-handle, when suddenly a loud noise and shouts were heard from the street. The distiller, who beside many other characteristics possessed a keen curiosity, laid down his pipe quickly and ran into the street; but the ne'er-do-wells had all dispersed.

"No, you don't escape me!" cried the headman, dragging someone muffled up in a sheepskin coat with the hair turned outwards, by the arm.

The distiller rapidly seized a favourable moment to look at the face of this disturber of the peace; but he started back when he saw a long beard and a grim, painted face.

"No, you don't escape me!" exclaimed the headman again as he dragged his prisoner into the vestibule.

The latter offered no resistance, and followed him as quietly as though it had been his own house.

"Karpo, open the store-room!" the headman called to the village councillor. "We will throw him in there! Then we will awake the clerk, call the village council together, catch this impudent rabble, and pass our sentence on them at once."

The village councillor unlocked the store-room; then in the darkness of the vestibule, the prisoner made a desperate effort to break loose from the headman's arms.

"Ah! you would, would you?" exclaimed the headman, holding him more firmly by the collar.

"Let me go! It is I!" a half-stifled voice was heard saying.

"It is no good, brother! You may squeal if you choose, like the devil, instead of imitating a woman, but you won't get round me." So saying, he thrust the prisoner with such violence into the dark room that he fell on the ground and groaned aloud.

The victorious headman, accompanied by the village councillor, now betook himself to the clerk's; they were followed by the distiller, who was veiled in clouds of tobacco-smoke, and resembled a steamer.

They were all three walking reflectively with bent heads, when suddenly, turning into a dark side-alley, they uttered a cry and started back in consequence of coming into collision with three other men, who on their side shouted with equal loudness. The headman saw with his one eye, to his no small astonishment, the clerk with two village councillors.

"I was just coming to you, Mr Notary."

"And I was on my way to your honour."

"These are strange goings-on, Mr Notary."

"Indeed they are, your honour."

"Have you seen them then?" asked the headman, surprised.

"The young fellows are roaming about the streets using vile language. They are abusing your honour in a way—in a word, it is a scandal. A drunken Russian would be ashamed to use such words."

The lean notary, in his gaily striped breeches and yeast-coloured waistcoat, kept on stretching forward and drawing back his neck while he talked.

"Hardly had I gone to sleep," he continued, "than the cursed loafers woke me up with their shameful songs and their noise. I meant to give them a sound rating, but while I was putting on my breeches and vest, they all ran away. But the ringleader has not escaped; for the present he is shut up in the hut which we use as a prison. I was very curious to know who the scapegrace is, but his face is as sooty as the devil's when he forges nails for sinners."

"What clothes does he wear, Mr Notary?"

"The son of a dog wears a black sheepskin coat turned inside out, your honour."

"Aren't you telling me a lie, Mr Notary? The same good-for-nothing is now shut up in my store-room under lock and key."

"No, your honour! You have drawn the long bow a little yourself, and should not be vexed at what I say."

"Bring a light! We will take a look at him at once!"

They returned to the headman's house; the store-room door was opened, and the headman groaned for sheer amazement as he saw his sister-in-law standing before him.

"Tell me then," she said, stepping forward, "have you quite lost your senses? Had you a single particle of brains in your one-eyed fish-head when you locked me up in the dark room? It is a mercy I did not break my head against the iron door hinge. Didn't I shout out that it was I? Then he seized me, the cursed bear, with his iron claws, and pushed me in. May Satan hereafter so push you into hell!" The last words she spoke from the street, having wisely gone out of his reach.

"Yes, now I see that it is you!" said the headman, who had slowly recovered his composure.

"Is he not a scamp and a scoundrel, Mr Clerk?" he continued.

"Yes, certainly, your honour."

"Isn't it high time to give all these loose fellows a lesson, that they may at last betake themselves to their work?"

"Yes, it is high time, your honour."

"The fools have combined in a gang. What the deuce is that? It sounded like my sister-in-law's voice. The blockheads think that I am like her, an ordinary Cossack."

Here he coughed and cleared his throat, and a gleam in his eyes showed that he was about to say something very important. "In the year one thousand—I cannot keep these cursed dates in my memory, if I was to be killed for it. Well, never mind when it was, the Commissary Ledatcho was commanded to choose out a Cossack who was cleverer than the rest. Yes," he added, raising his forefinger, "cleverer than the rest, to accompany the Czar. Then I was——"

"Yes, yes," the notary interrupted him, "we all know, headman, that you well deserved the imperial favour. But confess now that I was right: you made a mistake when you declared that you had caught the vagabond in the reversed sheepskin."

"This disguised devil I will have imprisoned to serve as a warning to the rest. They will have to learn what authority means. Who has appointed the headman, if not the Czar? Then we will tackle the other fellows. I don't forget how the scamps drove a whole herd of swine into my garden, which ate up all the cabbages and cucumbers; I don't forget how those sons of devils refused to thrash my rye for me. I don't forget—to the deuce with them! We must first find out who this scoundrel in the sheepskin really is."

"He is a sly dog anyway," said the distiller, whose cheeks during the whole conversation had been as full of smoke as a siege-cannon, and whose lips, when he took his pipe out of his mouth, seemed to emit sparks.

Meanwhile they had approached a small ruined hut. Their curiosity had mounted to the highest pitch, and they pressed round the door. The notary produced a key and tried to turn the lock, but it did not fit; it was the key of his trunk. The impatience of the onlookers increased. He plunged his hand into the wide pocket of his gaily striped breeches, bent his back, scraped with his feet, uttered imprecations, and at last cried triumphantly, "I have it!"

At these words the hearts of our heroes beat so loud, that the turning of the key in the lock was almost inaudible. At last the door opened, and the headman turned as white as a sheet. The distiller felt a shiver run down his spine, and his hair stood on end. Terror and apprehension were stamped on the notary's face; the village councillors almost sank into the ground and could not shut their wide-open mouths. Before them stood the headman's sister-in-law!

She was not less startled than they, but recovered herself somewhat, and made a movement as if to approach them.

"Stop!" cried the headman in an excited voice, and slammed the door again. "Sirs, Satan is behind this!" he continued. "Bring fire quickly! Never mind the hut! Set it alight and burn it up so that not even the witch's bones remain."

"Wait a minute, brother!" exclaimed the distiller. "Your hair is grey, but you are not very intelligent; no ordinary fire will burn a witch. Only the fire of a pipe can do it. I will manage it all right." So saying, he shook some glowing ashes from his pipe on to a bundle of straw, and began to fan the flame.

Despair gave the unfortunate woman courage; she began to implore them in a loud voice.

"Stop a moment, brother! Perhaps we are incurring guilt needlessly. Perhaps she is really no witch!" said the notary. "If the person sitting in there declares herself ready to make the sign of the cross, then she is not a child of the devil."

The proposal was accepted. "Look out, Satan!" continued the notary, speaking at a chink in the door. "If you promise not to move, we will open the door."

The door was opened.

"Cross yourself!" exclaimed the headman, looking round him for a safe place of retreat in case of necessity.

His sister-in-law crossed herself.

"The deuce! It is really you, sister-in-law!"

"What evil spirit dragged you into this hole, friend?" asked the notary.

The headman's sister related amid sobs how the rioters had seized her on the street, and in spite of her resistance, pushed her through a large window into the hut, on which they had closed the shutters. The notary looked and found that the bolt of the shutter had been wrenched off, and that it was held in its place by a wooden bar placed across it outside.

"You are a nice fellow, you one-eyed Satan!" she now exclaimed, advancing towards the headman, who stepped backwards and continued to contemplate her from head to foot. "I know your thoughts; you were glad of an opportunity to get me shut up in order to run after that petticoat, so that no one could see the grey-haired sinner making a fool of himself. You think I don't know how you talked this evening with Hanna. Oh, I know everything. You must get up earlier if you want to make a fool of me, you great stupid! I have endured for a long time, but at last don't take it ill if——"

She made a threatening gesture with her fist, and ran away swiftly, leaving the headman quite taken aback.

"The devil really has something to do with it!" he thought, rubbing his bald head.

"We have him!" now exclaimed the two village councillors as they approached.

"Whom have you?" asked the headman.

"The devil in the sheepskin."

"Bring him here!" cried the headman, seizing the prisoner by the arm. "Are you mad? This is the drunken Kalenik!"

"It is witchcraft! He was in our hands, your honour!" replied the village councillors. "The rascals were rushing about in the narrow side-streets, dancing and behaving like idiots—the devil take them! How it was we got hold of this fellow instead of him, heaven only knows!"

"In virtue of my authority, and that of the village assembly," said the headman, "I issue the order to seize these robbers and other young vagabonds which may be met with in the streets, and to bring them before me to be dealt with."

"Excuse us, your honour," answered the village councillors, bowing low. "If you could only see the hideous faces they had; may heaven punish us if ever anyone has seen such miscreations since he was born and baptised. These devils might frighten one into an illness."

"I'll teach you to be afraid! You won't obey then? You are certainly in the conspiracy with them! You mutineers! What is the meaning of that? What? You abet robbery and murder! You!—I will inform the Commissary. Go at once, do you hear; fly like birds. I shall—you will——"

They all dispersed in different directions.

V

THE DROWNED GIRL

Without troubling himself in the least about those who had been sent to pursue him, the originator of all this confusion slowly walked towards the old house and the pool. We hardly need to say it was Levko. His black fur coat was buttoned up; he carried his cap in his hand, and the perspiration was pouring down his face. The moon poured her light on the gloomy majesty of the dark maple-wood.

The coolness of the air round the motionless pool enticed the weary wanderer to rest by it a while. Universal silence prevailed, only that in the forest thickets the nightingales' songs were heard. An overpowering drowsiness closed his eyes; his tired limbs relaxed, and his head nodded.

"Ah! am I going to sleep?" he said, rising and rubbing his eyes.

He looked round; the night seemed to him still more beautiful. The moonlight seemed to have an intoxicating quality about it, a glamour which he had never perceived before. The landscape was veiled in a silver mist. The air was redolent with the perfume of the apple-blossoms and the night-flowers. Entranced, he gazed on the motionless pool. The old, half-ruined house was clearly reflected without a quiver in the water. But instead of dark shutters, he saw light streaming from brilliantly lit windows. Presently one of them opened. Holding his breath, and without moving a muscle, he fastened his eyes on the pool and seemed to penetrate its depths. What did he see? First he saw at the window a graceful, curly head with shining eyes, propped on a white arm; the head moved and smiled. His heart suddenly began to beat. The water began to break into ripples, and the window closed.

Quietly he withdrew from the pool, and looked towards the house. The dark shutters were flung back; the window-panes gleamed in the moonlight. "How little one can believe what people say!" he thought to himself. "The house is brand-new, and looks as though it had only just been painted. It is certainly inhabited."

He stepped nearer cautiously, but the house was quite silent. The clear song of the nightingales rose powerfully and distinctly on the air, and as they died away one heard the chirping and rustling of the grasshoppers, and the marshbird clapping his slippery beak in the water.

Levko felt enraptured with the sweetness and stillness of the night. He struck the strings of his guitar and sang:

"Oh lovely moon
Thou steepst in light
The house where my darling
Sleeps all night."

A window opened gently, and the same girl whose image he had seen in the pool looked out and listened attentively to

160

the song. Her long-lashed eyelids were partly drooping over her eyes; she was as pale as the moonlight, but wonderfully beautiful. She smiled, and a shiver ran through Levko.

"Sing me a song, young Cossack!" she said gently, bending her head sideways and quite closing her eyes.

"What song shall I sing you, dear girl?"

Tears rolled down her pale cheeks. "Cossack," she said, and there was something inexpressibly touching in her tone, "Cossack, find my stepmother for me. I will do everything for you; I will reward you; I will give you abundant riches. I have armlets embroidered with silk and coral necklaces; I will give you a girdle set with pearls. I have gold. Cossack, seek my stepmother for me. She is a terrible witch; she allowed me no peace in the beautiful world. She tortured me; she made me work like a common maid-servant. Look at my face; she has banished the redness from my cheeks with her unholy magic. Look at my white neck; they cannot be washed away, they cannot be washed away—the blue marks of her iron claws. Look at my white feet; they did not walk on carpets, but on hot sand, on damp ground, on piercing thorns. And my eyes—look at them; they are almost blind with weeping. Seek my stepmother!"

Her voice, which had gradually become louder, stopped, and she wept.

The Cossack felt overpowered by sympathy and grief. "I am ready to do everything to please you, dear lady," he cried with deep emotion; "but where and how can I find her?"

"Look, look!" she said quickly, "she is here! She dances on the lake-shore with my maidens, and warms herself in the moonlight. Yet she is cunning and sly. She has assumed the shape of one who is drowned, yet I know and hear that she is present. I am so afraid of her. Because of her I cannot swim free and light as a fish. I sink and fall to the bottom like a piece of iron. Look for her, Cossack!"

Levko cast a glance at the lake-shore. In a silvery mist there moved, like shadows, girls in white dresses decked with May flowers; gold necklaces and coins gleamed on their necks; but they were very pale, as though formed of transparent clouds. They danced nearer him, and he could hear their voices, somewhat like the sound of reeds stirred in the quiet evening by the breeze.

"Let us play the raven-game! Let us play the raven-game!"

"Who will be the raven?"

Lots were cast, and a girl stepped out of the line of the dancers.

Levko observed her attentively. Her face and clothing resembled those of the others; but she was evidently unwilling to play the part assigned her. The dancers revolved rapidly round her, without her being able to catch one of them.

"No, I won't be the raven any more," she said, quite exhausted. "I do not like to rob the poor mother-hen of her chickens."

"You are not a witch," thought Levko.

The girls again gathered together in order to cast lots who should be the raven.

"I will be the raven!" called one from the midst.

Levko watched her closely. Boldly and rapidly she ran after the dancers, and made every effort to catch her prey. Levko began to notice that her body was not transparent like the others; there was something black in the midst of it. Suddenly there was a cry; the "raven" had rushed on a girl, embraced her, and it seemed to Levko as though she had stretched out claws, and as though her face shone with malicious joy.

"Witch!" he cried out, pointing at her suddenly with his finger, and turning towards the house.

The girl at the window laughed, and the other girls dragged the "raven" screaming along with them.

"How shall I reward you, Cossack?" said the maiden. "I know you do not need gold; you love Hanna, but her harsh father will not allow you to marry. But give him this note, and he will cease to hinder it."

She stretched out her white hand, and her face shone wonderfully. With strange shudders and a beating heart, he grasped the paper and—awoke.

I

THE AWAKENING

"Have I then been really asleep?" Levko asked himself as he stood up. "Everything seemed so real, as though I were awake. Wonderful! Wonderful!" he repeated, looking round him. The position of the moon vertical overhead showed that it was midnight; a waft of coolness came from the pool. The ruined house with the closed shutters stood there with a melancholy aspect; the moss and weeds which grew thickly upon it showed that it had not been entered by any human foot for a long time. Then he suddenly opened his hand, which had been convulsively clenched during his sleep, and cried aloud with astonishment when he saw the note in it. "Ah! if I could only read," he thought, turning it this way and that. At that moment he heard a noise behind him.

"Fear nothing! Lay hold of him! What are you afraid of? There are ten of us. I wager that he is a man, and not the devil."

It was the headman encouraging his companions.

Levko felt himself seized by several arms, many of which were trembling with fear.

"Throw off your mask, friend! Cease trying to fool us," said the headman, taking him by the collar. But he started back when he saw him closely. "Levko! My son!" he exclaimed, letting his arms sink. "It is you, miserable boy! I thought some rascal, or disguised devil, was playing these tricks; but now it seems you have cooked this mess for your own father—placed yourself at the head of a band of robbers, and composed songs to ridicule him. Eh, Levko! What is the meaning of that? It seems your back is itching. Tie him fast!"

"Stop, father! I have been ordered to give you this note," said Levko.

"Let me see it then! But bind him all the same."

"Wait, headman," said the notary, unfolding the note; "it is the Commissary's handwriting!"

"The Commissary's?"

"The Commissary's?" echoed the village councillors mechanically.

"The Commissary's? Wonderful! Still more incomprehensible!" thought Levko.

"Read! Read!" said the headman. "What does the Commissary write?"

"Let us hear!" exclaimed the distiller, holding his pipe between his teeth, and lighting it.

The notary cleared his throat and began to read.

"'Order to the headman, Javtuk Makohonenko.

"'It has been brought to our knowledge that you, old id——'"

"Stop! Stop! That is unnecessary!" exclaimed the headman. "Even if I have not heard it, I know that that is not the chief matter. Read further!"

"'Consequently I order you at once to marry your son, Levko Makohonenko, to the Cossack's daughter, Hanna Petritchenka, to repair the bridges on the post-road, and to give no horses belonging to the lords of the manor to the county-court magistrates without my knowledge. If on my arrival I do not find these orders carried out, I shall hold you singly responsible.

"'Lieut. Kosma Derkatch-Drischpanowski,

"'*Commissary.*'"

"There we have it!" exclaimed the headman, with his mouth open. "Have you heard it? The headman is made responsible for everything, and therefore everyone has to obey him without contradiction! Otherwise, I beg to resign my office. And you," he continued, turning to Levko, "I will have married, as the Commissary directs, though it seems to me strange how he knows of the affair; but you will get a taste of my knout first—the one, you know, which hangs on the wall at my bed-head. But how did you get hold of the note?"

Levko, in spite of the astonishment which the unexpected turn of affairs caused him, had had the foresight to prepare an answer, and to conceal the way in which the note had come into his possession. "I was in the town last night," he said, "and met the Commissary just as he was alighting from his droshky. When he heard from which village I was he gave me the note and bid me tell you by word of mouth, father, that he would dine with us on his way back."

"Did he say that?"

"Yes."

"Have you heard it?" said the headman, with a solemn air turning to his companions. "The Commissary himself, in his own person, comes to us, that is to me, to dine." The headman lifted a finger and bent his head as though he were listening to something. "The Commissary, do you hear, the Commissary is coming to dine with me! What do you think, Mr Notary? And what do you think, friend? That is not a little honour, is it?"

"As far as I can recollect," the notary broke in, "no Commissary has ever dined with a headman."

"All headmen are not alike," he answered with a self-satisfied air. Then he uttered a hoarse laugh and said, "What do you think, Mr Notary? Isn't it right to order that in honour of the distinguished guest, a fowl, linen, and other things should be offered by every cottage?"

"Yes, they should."

"And when is the wedding to be, father?" asked Levko.

"Wedding! I should like to celebrate your wedding in my way! Well, in honour of the distinguished guest, to-morrow the pope(1) will marry you. Let the Commissary see that you are punctual. Now, children, we will go to bed. Go to your houses. The present occasion reminds me of the time when I——" At these words the headman assumed his customary solemn air.

"Now the headman will relate how he accompanied the Czarina!" said Levko to himself, and hastened quickly, and full of joy, to the cherry-tree-shaded house, which we know. "May God bless you, beloved, and the holy angels smile on you. To no one will I relate the wonders of this night except to you, Hanna; you alone will believe it, and pray with me for the repose of the souls of the poor drowned maidens."

He approached the house; the window was open; the moonbeams fell on Hanna, who was sleeping by it. Her head was supported on her arm; her cheeks glowed; her lips moved, gently murmuring his name.

"Sleep sweetly, my darling. Dream of everything that is good, and yet the awaking will surpass all." He made the sign of the cross over her, closed the window, and gently withdrew.

In a few moments the whole village was buried in slumber. Only the moon hung as brilliant and wonderful as before in the immensity of the Ukraine sky. The divine night continued her reign in solemn stillness, while the earth lay bathed in silvery radiance. The universal silence was only broken here and there by the bark of a dog; only the drunken Kalenik still wandered about the empty streets seeking for his house.

THE VIY

(The "Viy" is a monstrous creation of popular fancy. It is the name which the inhabitants of Little Russia give to the king of the gnomes, whose eyelashes reach to the ground. The following story is a specimen of such folk-lore. I have made no alterations, but reproduce it in the same simple form in which I heard it.—Author's Note.)

I

As soon as the clear seminary bell began sounding in Kieff in the morning, the pupils would come flocking from all parts of the town. The students of grammar, rhetoric, philosophy, and theology hastened with their books under their arms over the streets.

The "grammarians" were still mere boys. On the way they pushed against each other and quarrelled with shrill voices. Nearly all of them wore torn or dirty clothes, and their pockets were always crammed with all kinds of things—push-bones, pipes made out of pens, remains of confectionery, and sometimes even young sparrows. The latter would sometimes begin to chirp in the midst of deep silence in the school, and bring down on their possessors severe canings and thrashings.

The "rhetoricians" walked in a more orderly way. Their clothes were generally untorn, but on the other hand their faces were often strangely decorated; one had a black eye, and the lips of another resembled a single blister, etc. These spoke to each other in tenor voices.

The "philosophers" talked in a tone an octave lower; in their pockets they only had fragments of tobacco, never whole cakes of it; for what they could get hold of, they used at once. They smelt so strongly of tobacco and brandy, that a workman passing by them would often remain standing and sniffing with his nose in the air, like a hound.

About this time of day the market-place was generally full of bustle, and the market women, selling rolls, cakes, and honey-tarts, plucked the sleeves of those who wore coats of fine cloth or cotton.

"Young sir! Young sir! Here! Here!" they cried from all sides. "Rolls and cakes and tasty tarts, very delicious! I have baked them myself!"

Another drew something long and crooked out of her basket and cried, "Here is a sausage, young sir! Buy a sausage!"

"Don't buy anything from her!" cried a rival. "See how greasy she is, and what a dirty nose and hands she has!"

But the market women carefully avoided appealing to the philosophers and theologians, for these only took handfuls of eatables merely to taste them.

Arrived at the seminary, the whole crowd of students dispersed into the low, large class-rooms with small windows, broad doors, and blackened benches. Suddenly they were filled with a many-toned murmur. The teachers heard the pupils' lessons repeated, some in shrill and others in deep voices which sounded like a distant booming. While the lessons were being said, the teachers kept a sharp eye open to see whether pieces of cake or other dainties were protruding from their pupils' pockets; if so, they were promptly confiscated.

When this learned crowd arrived somewhat earlier than usual, or when it was known that the teachers would come somewhat late, a battle would ensue, as though planned by general agreement. In this battle all had to take part, even the monitors who were appointed to look after the order and morality of the whole school. Two theologians generally arranged the conditions of the battle: whether each class should split into two sides, or whether all the pupils should divide themselves into two halves.

In each case the grammarians began the battle, and after the rhetoricians had joined in, the former retired and stood on the benches, in order to watch the fortunes of the fray. Then came the philosophers with long black moustaches, and finally the thick-necked theologians. The battle generally ended in a victory for the latter, and the philosophers retired to the different class-rooms rubbing their aching limbs, and throwing themselves on the benches to take breath.

When the teacher, who in his own time had taken part in such contests, entered the class-room he saw by the heated faces of his pupils that the battle had been very severe, and while he caned the hands of the rhetoricians, in another room another teacher did the same for the philosophers.

On Sundays and Festival Days the seminarists took puppet-theatres to the citizens' houses. Sometimes they acted a comedy, and in that case it was always a theologian who took the part of the hero or heroine—Potiphar or Herodias, etc. As a reward for their exertions, they received a piece of linen, a sack of maize, half a roast goose, or something similar. All the students, lay and clerical, were very poorly provided with means for procuring themselves necessary subsistence, but at the same time very fond of eating; so that, however much food was given to them, they were never satisfied, and the gifts bestowed by rich landowners were never adequate for their needs.

Therefore the Commissariat Committee, consisting of philosophers and theologians, sometimes dispatched the grammarians and rhetoricians under the leadership of a philosopher—themselves sometimes joining in the expedition—with sacks on their shoulders, into the town, in order to levy a contribution on the fleshpots of the citizens, and then there was a feast in the seminary.

The most important event in the seminary year was the arrival of the holidays; these began in July, and then generally all the students went home. At that time all the roads were thronged with grammarians, rhetoricians, philosophers, and theologians. He who had no home of his own, would take up his quarters with some fellow-student's family; the philosophers and theologians looked out for tutors' posts, taught the children of rich farmers, and received for doing so a pair of new boots and sometimes also a new coat.

A whole troop of them would go off in close ranks like a regiment; they cooked their porridge in common, and encamped under the open sky. Each had a bag with him containing a shirt and a pair of socks. The theologians were especially economical; in order not to wear out their boots too quickly, they took them off and carried them on a stick over their shoulders, especially when the road was very muddy. Then they tucked up their breeches over their knees and waded bravely through the pools and puddles. Whenever they spied a village near the highway, they at once left it, approached the house which seemed the most considerable, and began with loud voices to sing a psalm. The master of the house, an old Cossack engaged in agriculture, would listen for a long time with his head propped in his hands, then with tears on his cheeks say to his wife, "What the students are singing sounds very devout; bring out some lard and anything else of the kind we have in the house."

After thus replenishing their stores, the students would continue their way. The farther they went, the smaller grew their numbers, as they dispersed to their various houses, and left those whose homes were still farther on.

On one occasion, during such a march, three students left the main-road in order to get provisions in some village, since their stock had long been exhausted. This party consisted of the theologian Khalava, the philosopher Thomas Brutus, and the rhetorician Tiberius Gorobetz.

The first was a tall youth with broad shoulders and of a peculiar character; everything which came within reach of his fingers he felt obliged to appropriate. Moreover, he was of a very melancholy disposition, and when he had got intoxicated he hid himself in the most tangled thickets so that the seminary officials had the greatest trouble in finding him.

The philosopher Thomas Brutus was a more cheerful character. He liked to lie for a long time on the same spot and smoke his pipe; and when he was merry with wine, he hired a fiddler and danced the "tropak." Often he got a whole quantity of "beans," i.e. thrashings; but these he endured with complete philosophic calm, saying that a man cannot escape his destiny.

174

The rhetorician Tiberius Gorobetz had not yet the right to wear a moustache, to drink brandy, or to smoke tobacco. He only wore a small crop of hair, as though his character was at present too little developed. To judge by the great bumps on his forehead, with which he often appeared in the class-room, it might be expected that some day he would be a valiant fighter. Khalava and Thomas often pulled his hair as a mark of their special favour, and sent him on their errands.

Evening had already come when they left the high-road; the sun had just gone down, and the air was still heavy with the heat of the day. The theologian and the philosopher strolled along, smoking in silence, while the rhetorician struck off the heads of the thistles by the wayside with his stick. The way wound on through thick woods of oak and walnut; green hills alternated here and there with meadows. Twice already they had seen cornfields, from which they concluded that they were near some village; but an hour had already passed, and no human habitation appeared. The sky was already quite dark, and only a red gleam lingered on the western horizon.

"The deuce!" said the philosopher Thomas Brutus. "I was almost certain we would soon reach a village."

The theologian still remained silent, looked round him, then put his pipe again between his teeth, and all three continued their way.

"Good heavens!" exclaimed the philosopher, and stood still. "Now the road itself is disappearing."

"Perhaps we shall find a farm farther on," answered the theologian, without taking his pipe out of his mouth.

Meanwhile the night had descended; clouds increased the darkness, and according to all appearance there was no chance of moon or stars appearing. The seminarists found that they had lost the way altogether.

After the philosopher had vainly sought for a footpath, he exclaimed, "Where have we got to?"

The theologian thought for a while, and said, "Yes, it is really dark."

The rhetorician went on one side, lay on the ground, and groped for a path; but his hands encountered only fox-holes. All around lay a huge steppe over which no one seemed to have passed. The wanderers made several efforts to get forward, but the landscape grew wilder and more inhospitable.

The philosopher tried to shout, but his voice was lost in vacancy, no one answered; only, some moments later, they heard a faint groaning sound, like the whimpering of a wolf.

"Curse it all! What shall we do?" said the philosopher.

"Why, just stop here, and spend the night in the open air," answered the theologian. So saying, he felt in his pocket, brought out his timber and steel, and lit his pipe.

But the philosopher could not agree with this proposal; he was not accustomed to sleep till he had first eaten five pounds of bread and five of dripping, and so he now felt an intolerable emptiness in his stomach. Besides, in spite of his cheerful temperament, he was a little afraid of the wolves.

"No, Khalava," he said, "that won't do. To lie down like a dog and without any supper! Let us try once more; perhaps we shall find a house, and the consolation of having a glass of brandy to drink before going to sleep."

At the word "brandy," the theologian spat on one side and said, "Yes, of course, we cannot remain all night in the open air."

The students went on and on, and to their great joy they heard the barking of dogs in the distance. After listening a while to see from which direction the barking came, they went on their way with new courage, and soon espied a light.

"A village, by heavens, a village!" exclaimed the philosopher.

His supposition proved correct; they soon saw two or three houses built round a court-yard. Lights glimmered in the windows, and before the fence stood a number of trees. The students looked through the crevices of the gates and saw a court-yard in which stood a large number of roving tradesmen's carts. In the sky there were now fewer clouds, and here and there a star was visible.

"See, brother!" one of them said, "we must now cry 'halt!' Cost what it may, we must find entrance and a night's lodging."

The three students knocked together at the gate, and cried "Open!"

The door of one of the houses creaked on its hinges, and an old woman wrapped in a sheepskin appeared. "Who is there?" she exclaimed, coughing loudly.

"Let us spend the night here, mother; we have lost our way, our stomachs are empty, and we do not want to spend the night out of doors."

"But what sort of people are you?"

"Quite harmless people; the theologian Khalava, the philosopher Brutus, and the rhetorician Gorobetz."

"It is impossible," answered the old woman. "The whole house is full of people, and every corner occupied. Where can I put you up? You are big and heavy enough to break the house down. I know these philosophers and theologians; when once one takes them in, they eat one out of house and home. Go farther on! There is no room here for you!"

"Have pity on us, mother! How can you be so heartless? Don't let Christians perish. Put us up where you like, and if we eat up your provisions, or do any other damage, may our hands wither up, and all the punishment of heaven light on us!"

The old woman seemed a little touched. "Well," she said after a few moments' consideration, "I will let you in; but I must put you in different rooms, for I should have no quiet if you were all together at night."

"Do just as you like; we won't say any more about it," answered the students.

The gates moved heavily on their hinges, and they entered the court-yard.

"Well now, mother," said the philosopher, following the old woman, "if you had a little scrap of something! By heavens! my stomach is as empty as a drum. I have not had a bit of bread in my mouth since early this morning!"

"Didn't I say so?" replied the old woman. "There you go begging at once. But I have no food in the house, nor any fire."

"But we will pay for everything," continued the philosopher.

"We will pay early to-morrow in cash."

"Go on and be content with what you get. You are fine fellows whom the devil has brought here!"

Her reply greatly depressed the philosopher Thomas; but suddenly his nose caught the odour of dried fish; he looked at the breeches of the theologian, who walked by his side, and saw a huge fish's tail sticking out of his pocket. The latter had already seized the opportunity to steal a whole fish from one of the carts standing in the court-yard. He had not done this from hunger so much as from the force of habit. He had quite forgotten the fish, and was looking about to see whether he could not find something else to appropriate. Then the philosopher put his hand in the theologian's pocket as though it were his own, and laid hold of his prize.

The old woman found a special resting-place for each student; the rhetorician she put in a shed, the theologian in an empty store-room, and the philosopher in a sheep's stall.

As soon as the philosopher was alone, he devoured the fish in a twinkling, examined the fence which enclosed the stall, kicked away a pig from a neighbouring stall, which had inquiringly inserted its nose through a crevice, and lay down on his right side to sleep like a corpse.

Then the low door opened, and the old woman came crouching into the stall.

"Well, mother, what do you want here?" asked the philosopher.

She made no answer, but came with outstretched arms towards him.

The philosopher shrank back; but she still approached, as though she wished to lay hold of him. A terrible fright seized him, for he saw the old hag's eyes sparkle in an extraordinary way. "Away with you, old witch, away with you!" he shouted. But she still stretched her hands after him.

He jumped up in order to rush out, but she placed herself before the door, fixed her glowing eyes upon him, and again approached him. The philosopher tried to push her away with his hands, but to his astonishment he found that he could neither lift his hands nor move his legs, nor utter an audible word. He only heard his heart beating, and saw the old woman approach him, place his hands crosswise on his breast, and bend his head down. Then with the agility of a cat she sprang on his shoulders, struck him on the side with a broom, and he began to run like a race-horse, carrying her on his shoulders.

All this happened with such swiftness, that the philosopher could scarcely collect his thoughts. He laid hold of his knees with both hands in order to stop his legs from running; but to his great astonishment they kept moving forward against his will, making rapid springs like a Caucasian horse.

Not till the house had been left behind them and a wide plain stretched before them, bordered on one side by a black gloomy wood, did he say to himself, "Ah! it is a witch!"

The half-moon shone pale and high in the sky. Its mild light, still more subdued by intervening clouds, fell like a transparent veil on the earth. Woods, meadows, hills, and valleys—all seemed to be sleeping with open eyes; nowhere was a breath of air stirring. The atmosphere was moist and warm; the shadows of the trees and bushes fell sharply defined on the sloping plain. Such was the night through which the philosopher Thomas Brutus sped with his strange rider.

A strange, oppressive, and yet sweet sensation took possession of his heart. He looked down and saw how the grass beneath his feet seemed to be quite deep and far away; over it there flowed a flood of crystal-clear water, and the grassy plain looked like the bottom of a transparent sea. He saw his own image, and that of the old woman whom he carried on his back, clearly reflected in it. Then he beheld how, instead of the moon, a strange sun shone there; he heard the deep tones of bells, and saw them swinging. He saw a water-nixie rise from a bed of tall reeds; she turned to him, and her face was clearly visible, and she sang a song which penetrated his soul; then she approached him and nearly reached the surface of the water, on which she burst into laughter and again disappeared.

Did he see it or did he not see it? Was he dreaming or was he awake? But what was that below—wind or music? It sounded and drew nearer, and penetrated his soul like a song that rose and fell. "What is it?" he thought as he gazed into the depths, and still sped rapidly along.

The perspiration flowed from him in streams; he experienced simultaneously a strange feeling of oppression and delight in all his being. Often he felt as though he had no longer a heart, and pressed his hand on his breast with alarm.

Weary to death, he began to repeat all the prayers which he knew, and all the formulas of exorcism against evil spirits. Suddenly he experienced a certain relief. He felt that his pace was slackening; the witch weighed less heavily on his shoulders, and the thick herbage of the plain was again beneath his feet, with nothing especial to remark about it.

"Splendid!" thought the philosopher Thomas, and began to repeat his exorcisms in a still louder voice.

Then suddenly he wrenched himself away from under the witch, and sprang on her back in his turn. She began to run, with short, trembling steps indeed, but so rapidly that he could hardly breathe. So swiftly did she run that she hardly seemed to touch the ground. They were still on the plain, but owing to the rapidity of their flight everything seemed indistinct and confused before his eyes. He seized a stick that was lying on the ground, and began to belabour the hag with all his might. She uttered a wild cry, which at first sounded raging and threatening; then it became gradually weaker and more gentle, till at last it sounded quite low like the pleasant tones of a silver bell, so that it penetrated his innermost soul. Involuntarily the thought passed through his mind:

"Is she really an old woman?"

"Ah! I can go no farther," she said in a faint voice, and sank to the earth.

He knelt beside her, and looked in her eyes. The dawn was red in the sky, and in the distance glimmered the gilt domes of the churches of Kieff. Before him lay a beautiful maiden with thick, dishevelled hair and long eyelashes. Unconsciously she had stretched out her white, bare arms, and her tear-filled eyes gazed at the sky.

Thomas trembled like an aspen-leaf. Sympathy, and a strange feeling of excitement, and a hitherto unknown fear overpowered him. He began to run with all his might. His heart beat violently, and he could not explain to himself what a strange, new feeling had seized him. He did not wish to return to the village, but hastened towards Kieff, thinking all the way as he went of his weird, unaccountable adventure.

There were hardly any students left in the town; they were all scattered about the country, and had either taken tutors' posts or simply lived without occupation; for at the farms in Little Russia one can live comfortably and at ease without paying a farthing. The great half-decayed building in which the seminary was established was completely empty; and however much the philosopher searched in all its corners for a piece of lard and bread, he could not find even one of the hard biscuits which the seminarists were in the habit of hiding.

But the philosopher found a means of extricating himself from his difficulties by making friends with a certain young widow in the market-place who sold ribbons, etc. The same evening he found himself being stuffed with cakes and fowl; in fact it is impossible to say how many things were placed before him on a little table in an arbour shaded by cherry-trees.

Later on the same evening the philosopher was to be seen in an ale-house. He lay on a bench, smoked his pipe in his usual way, and threw the Jewish publican a gold piece. He had a jug of ale standing before him, looked on all who went in and out in a cold-blooded, self-satisfied way, and thought no more of his strange adventure.

. . . . . .

About this time a report spread about that the daughter of a rich colonel, whose estate lay about fifty versts distant from Kieff, had returned home one day from a walk in a quite broken-down condition. She had scarcely enough strength to reach her father's house; now she lay dying, and had expressed a wish that for three days after her death the prayers for the dead should be recited by a Kieff seminarist named Thomas Brutus.

This fact was communicated to the philosopher by the rector of the seminary himself, who sent for him to his room and told him that he must start at once, as a rich colonel had sent his servants and a kibitka for him. The philosopher trembled, and was seized by an uncomfortable feeling which he could not define. He had a gloomy foreboding that some evil was about to befall him. Without knowing why, he declared that he did not wish to go.

185

"Listen, Thomas," said the rector, who under certain circumstances spoke very politely to his pupils; "I have no idea of asking you whether you wish to go or not. I only tell you that if you think of disobeying, I will have you so soundly flogged on the back with young birch-rods, that you need not think of having a bath for a long time."

The philosopher scratched the back of his head, and went out silently, intending to make himself scarce at the first opportunity. Lost in thought, he descended the steep flight of steps which led to the court-yard, thickly planted with poplars; there he remained standing for a moment, and heard quite distinctly the rector giving orders in a loud voice to his steward, and to another person, probably one of the messengers sent by the colonel.

"Thank your master for the peeled barley and the eggs," said the rector; "and tell him that as soon as the books which he mentions in his note are ready, I will send them. I have already given them to a clerk to be copied. And don't forget to remind your master that he has some excellent fish, especially prime sturgeon, in his ponds; he might send me some when he has the opportunity, as here in the market the fish are bad and dear. And you, Jantukh, give the colonel's man a glass of brandy. And mind you tie up the philosopher, or he will show you a clean pair of heels."

"Listen to the scoundrel!" thought the philosopher. "He has smelt a rat, the long-legged stork!"

He descended into the court-yard and beheld there a kibitka, which he at first took for a barn on wheels. It was, in fact, as roomy as a kiln, so that bricks might have been made inside it. It was one of those remarkable Cracow vehicles in which Jews travelled from town to town in scores, wherever they thought they would find a market. Six stout, strong, though somewhat elderly Cossacks were standing by it. Their gold-braided coats of fine cloth showed that their master was rich and of some importance; and certain little scars testified to their valour on the battle-field.

"What can I do?" thought the philosopher. "There is no escaping one's destiny." So he stepped up to the Cossacks and said "Good day, comrades."

"Welcome, Mr Philosopher!" some of them answered.

"Well, I am to travel with you! It is a magnificent vehicle," he continued as he got into it. "If there were only musicians present, one might dance in it."

"Yes, it is a roomy carriage," said one of the Cossacks, taking his seat by the coachman. The latter had tied a cloth round his head, as he had already found an opportunity of pawning his cap in the ale-house. The other five, with the philosopher, got into the capacious kibitka, and sat upon sacks which were filled with all sorts of articles purchased in the city.

"I should like to know," said the philosopher, "if this equipage were laden with salt or iron, how many horses would be required to draw it?"

"Yes," said the Cossack who sat by the coachman, after thinking a short time, "it would require a good many horses."

After giving this satisfactory answer, the Cossack considered himself entitled to remain silent for the whole of the rest of the journey.

The philosopher would gladly have found out who the colonel was, and what sort of a character he had. He was also curious to know about his daughter, who had returned home in such a strange way and now lay dying, and whose destiny seemed to be mingled with his own; and wanted to know the sort of life that was lived in the colonel's house. But the Cossacks were probably philosophers like himself, for in answer to his inquiries they only blew clouds of tobacco and settled themselves more comfortably on their sacks.

Meanwhile, one of them addressed to the coachman on the box a brief command: "Keep your eyes open, Overko, you old sleepy-head, and when you come to the ale-house on the road to Tchukrailoff, don't forget to pull up and wake me and the other fellows if we are asleep." Then he began to snore pretty loud. But in any case his admonition was quite superfluous; for scarcely had the enormous equipage begun to approach the aforesaid ale-house, than they all cried with one mouth "Halt! Halt!" Besides this, Overko's horse was accustomed to stop outside every inn of its own accord.

In spite of the intense July heat, they all got out and entered a low, dirty room where a Jewish innkeeper received them in a friendly way as old acquaintances. He brought in the skirt of his long coat some sausages, and laid them on the table, where, though forbidden by the Talmud, they looked very seductive. All sat down at table, and it was not long before each of the guests had an earthenware jug standing in front of him. The philosopher Thomas had to take part in the feast, and as the Little Russians when they are intoxicated always begin to kiss each other or to weep, the whole room soon began to echo with demonstrations of affection.

"Come here, come here, Spirid, let me embrace thee!"

"Come here, Dorosch, let me press you to my heart!"

One Cossack, with a grey moustache, the eldest of them all, leant his head on his hand and began to weep bitterly because he was an orphan and alone in God's wide world. Another tall, loquacious man did his best to comfort him, saying, "Don't weep, for God's sake, don't weep! For over there—God knows best."

The Cossack who had been addressed as Dorosch was full of curiosity, and addressed many questions to the philosopher Thomas. "I should like to know," he said, "what you learn in your seminary; do you learn the same things as the deacon reads to us in church, or something else?"

"Don't ask," said the consoler; "let them learn what they like. God knows what is to happen; God knows everything."

"No, I will know," answered Dorosch, "I will know what is written in their books; perhaps it is something quite different from that in the deacon's book."

"O good heavens!" said the other, "why all this talk? It is God's will, and one cannot change God's arrangements."

"But I will know everything that is written; I will enter the seminary too, by heaven I will! Do you think perhaps I could not learn? I will learn everything, everything."

"Oh, heavens!" exclaimed the consoler, and let his head sink on the table, for he could no longer hold it upright.

The other Cossacks talked about the nobility, and why there was a moon in the sky.

When the philosopher Thomas saw the state they were in, he determined to profit by it, and to make his escape. In the first place he turned to the grey-headed Cossack, who was lamenting the loss of his parents. "But, little uncle," he said to him, "why do you weep so? I too am an orphan! Let me go, children; why do you want me?"

"Let him go!" said some of them, "he is an orphan, let him go where he likes."

They were about to take him outside themselves, when the one who had displayed a special thirst for knowledge, stopped them, saying, "No, I want to talk with him about the seminary; I am going to the seminary myself."

Moreover, it was not yet certain whether the philosopher could have executed his project of flight, for when he tried to rise from his chair, he felt as though his feet were made of wood, and he began to see such a number of doors leading out of the room that it would have been difficult for him to have found the right one.

It was not till evening that the company remembered that they must continue their journey. They crowded into the kibitka, whipped up the horses, and struck up a song, the words and sense of which were hard to understand. During a great part of the night, they wandered about, having lost the road which they ought to have been able to find blindfolded. At last they drove down a steep descent into a valley, and the philosopher noticed, by the sides of the road, hedges, behind which he caught glimpses of small trees and house-roofs. All these belonged to the colonel's estate.

It was already long past midnight. The sky was dark, though little stars glimmered here and there; no light was to be seen in any of the houses. They drove into a large court-yard, while the dogs barked. On all sides were barns and cottages with thatched roofs. Just opposite the gateway was a house, which was larger than the others, and seemed to be the colonel's dwelling. The kibitka stopped before a small barn, and the travellers hastened into it and laid themselves down to sleep. The philosopher however attempted to look at the exterior of the house, but, rub his eyes as he might, he could distinguish nothing; the house seemed to turn into a bear, and the chimney into the rector of the seminary. Then he gave it up and lay down to sleep.

When he woke up the next morning, the whole house was in commotion; the young lady had died during the night. The servants ran hither and thither in a distracted state; the old women wept and lamented; and a number of curious people gazed through the enclosure into the court-yard, as though there were something special to be seen. The philosopher began now to inspect the locality and the buildings, which he had not been able to do during the night.

The colonel's house was one of those low, small buildings, such as used formerly to be constructed in Russia. It was thatched with straw; a small, high-peaked gable, with a window shaped like an eye, was painted all over with blue and yellow flowers and red crescent-moons; it rested on little oaken pillars, which were round above the middle, hexagonal below, and whose capitals were adorned with quaint carvings. Under this gable was a small staircase with seats at the foot of it on either side.

The walls of the house were supported by similar pillars. Before the house stood a large pear-tree of pyramidal shape, whose leaves incessantly trembled. A double row of buildings formed a broad street leading up to the colonel's house. Behind the barns near the entrance-gate stood two three-cornered wine-houses, also thatched with straw; each of the stone walls had a door in it, and was covered with all kinds of paintings. On one was represented a Cossack sitting on a barrel and swinging a large pitcher over his head; it bore the inscription "I will drink all that!" Elsewhere were painted large and small bottles, a beautiful girl, a running horse, a pipe, and a drum bearing the words "Wine is the Cossack's joy."

In the loft of one of the barns one saw through a huge round window a drum and some trumpets. At the gate there stood two cannons. All this showed that the colonel loved a cheerful life, and the whole place often rang with sounds of merriment. Before the gate were two windmills, and behind the house gardens sloped away; through the tree-tops the dark chimneys of the peasants' houses were visible. The whole village lay on a broad, even plateau, in the middle of a mountain-slope which culminated in a steep summit on the north side. When seen from below, it looked still steeper. Here and there on the top the irregular stems of the thick steppe-brooms showed in dark relief against the blue sky. The bare clay soil made a melancholy impression, worn as it was into deep furrows by rain-water. On the same slope there stood two cottages, and over one of them a huge apple-tree spread its branches; the roots were supported by small props, whose interstices were filled with mould. The apples, which were blown off by the wind, rolled down to the court-yard below. A road wound round the mountain to the village.

When the philosopher looked at this steep slope, and remembered his journey of the night before, he came to the conclusion that either the colonel's horses were very sagacious, or that the Cossacks must have very strong heads, as they ventured, even when the worse for drink, on such a road with the huge kibitka.

When the philosopher turned and looked in the opposite direction, he saw quite another picture. The village reached down to the plain; meadows stretched away to an immense distance, their bright green growing gradually dark; far away, about twenty versts off, many other villages were visible. To the right of these meadows were chains of hills, and in the remote distance one saw the Dnieper shimmer and sparkle like a mirror of steel.

"What a splendid country!" said the philosopher to himself. "It must be fine to live here! One could catch fish in the Dnieper, and in the ponds, and shoot and snare partridges and bustards; there must be quantities here. Much fruit might be dried here and sold in the town, or, better still, brandy might be distilled from it, for fruit-brandy is the best of all. But what prevents me thinking of my escape after all?"

Behind the hedge he saw a little path which was almost entirely concealed by the high grass of the steppe. The philosopher approached it mechanically, meaning at first to walk a little along it unobserved, and then quite quietly to gain the open country behind the peasants' houses. Suddenly he felt the pressure of a fairly heavy hand on his shoulder.

Behind him stood the same old Cossack who yesterday had so bitterly lamented the death of his father and mother, and his own loneliness. "You are giving yourself useless trouble, Mr Philosopher, if you think you can escape from us," he said. "One cannot run away here; and besides, the roads are too bad for walkers. Come to the colonel; he has been waiting for you for some time in his room."

"Yes, of course! What are you talking about? I will come with the greatest pleasure," said the philosopher, and followed the Cossack.

The colonel was an elderly man; his moustache was grey, and his face wore the signs of deep sadness. He sat in his room by a table, with his head propped on both hands. He seemed about five-and-fifty, but his attitude of utter despair, and the pallor on his face, showed that his heart had been suddenly broken, and that all his former cheerfulness had for ever disappeared.

When Thomas entered with the Cossack, he answered their deep bows with a slight inclination of the head.

"Who are you, whence do you come, and what is your profession, my good man?" asked the colonel in an even voice, neither friendly nor austere.

"I am a student of philosophy; my name is Thomas Brutus."

"And who was your father?"

"I don't know, sir."

"And your mother?"

"I don't know either; I know that I must have had a mother, but who she was, and where she lived, by heavens, I do not know."

The colonel was silent, and seemed for a moment lost in thought. "Where did you come to know my daughter?"

"I do not know her, gracious sir; I declare I do not know her."

"Why then has she chosen you, and no one else, to offer up prayers for her?"

The philosopher shrugged his shoulders. "God only knows. It is a well-known fact that grand people often demand things which the most learned man cannot comprehend; and does not the proverb say, 'Dance, devil, as the Lord commands!'"

"Aren't you talking nonsense, Mr Philosopher?"

"May the lightning strike me on the spot if I lie."

"If she had only lived a moment longer," said the colonel sadly, "then I had certainly found out everything. She said,

'Let no one offer up prayers for me, but send, father, at once to the seminary in Kieff for the student Thomas Brutus; he shall pray three nights running for my sinful soul—he knows.' But what he really knows she never said. The poor dove could speak no more, and died. Good man, you are probably well known for your sanctity and devout life, and she has perhaps heard of you."

"What? Of me?" said the philosopher, and took a step backward in amazement. "I and sanctity!" he exclaimed, and stared at the colonel. "God help us, gracious sir! What are you saying? It was only last Holy Thursday that I paid a visit to the tart-shop."

"Well, she must at any rate have had some reason for making the arrangement, and you must begin your duties to-day."

"I should like to remark to your honour—naturally everyone who knows the Holy Scripture at all can in his measure—but I believe it would be better on this occasion to send for a deacon or subdeacon. They are learned people, and they know exactly what is to be done. I have not got a good voice, nor any official standing."

"You may say what you like, but I shall carry out all my dove's wishes. If you read the prayers for her three nights through in the proper way, I will reward you; and if not—I advise the devil himself not to oppose me!"

The colonel spoke the last words in such an emphatic way that the philosopher quite understood them.

"Follow me!" said the colonel.

They went into the hall. The colonel opened a door which was opposite his own. The philosopher remained for a few minutes in the hall in order to look about him; then he stepped over the threshold with a certain nervousness.

The whole floor of the room was covered with red cloth. In a corner under the icons of the saints, on a table covered with a gold-bordered, velvet cloth, lay the body of the girl. Tall candles, round which were wound branches of the "calina," stood at her head and feet, and burned dimly in the broad daylight. The face of the dead was not to be seen, as the inconsolable father sat before his daughter, with his back turned to the philosopher. The words which the latter overheard filled him with a certain fear:

"I do not mourn, my daughter, that in the flower of your age you have prematurely left the earth, to my grief; but I mourn, my dove, that I do not know my deadly enemy who caused your death. Had I only known that anyone could even conceive the idea of insulting you, or of speaking a disrespectful word to you, I swear by heaven he would never have seen his children again, if he had been as old as myself; nor his father and mother, if he had been young. And I would have thrown his corpse to the birds of the air, and the wild beasts of the steppe. But woe is me, my flower,

my dove, my light! I will spend the remainder of my life
without joy, and wipe the bitter tears which flow out of my
old eyes, while my enemy will rejoice and laugh in secret
over the helpless old man!"

He paused, overpowered by grief, and streams of tears
flowed down his cheeks.

The philosopher was deeply affected by the sight of such
inconsolable sorrow. He coughed gently in order to clear his
throat. The colonel turned and signed to him to take his
place at the head of the dead girl, before a little prayer-desk
on which some books lay.

"I can manage to hold out for three nights," thought
the philosopher; "and then the colonel will fill both my
pockets with ducats."

He approached the dead girl, and after coughing once
more, began to read, without paying attention to anything
else, and firmly resolved not to look at her face.

Soon there was deep silence, and he saw that the colonel
had left the room. Slowly he turned his head in order to look
at the corpse. A violent shudder thrilled through him; before
him lay a form of such beauty as is seldom seen upon earth.
It seemed to him that never in a single face had so much
intensity of expression and harmony of feature been united.
Her brow, soft as snow and pure as silver, seemed to be
thinking; the fine, regular eyebrows shadowed proudly the
closed eyes, whose lashes gently rested on her cheeks, which

seemed to glow with secret longing; her lips still appeared to smile. But at the same time he saw something in these features which appalled him; a terrible depression seized his heart, as when in the midst of dance and song someone begins to chant a dirge. He felt as though those ruby lips were coloured with his own heart's blood. Moreover, her face seemed dreadfully familiar.

"The witch!" he cried out in a voice which sounded strange to himself; then he turned away and began to read the prayers with white cheeks. It was the witch whom he had killed.

II

When the sun had sunk below the horizon, the corpse was carried into the church. The philosopher supported one corner of the black-draped coffin upon his shoulder, and felt an ice-cold shiver run through his body. The colonel walked in front of him, with his right hand resting on the edge of the coffin.

The wooden church, black with age and overgrown with green lichen, stood quite at the end of the village in gloomy solitude; it was adorned with three round cupolas. One saw at the first glance that it had not been used for divine worship for a long time.

Lighted candles were standing before almost every icon. The coffin was set down before the altar. The old colonel kissed his dead daughter once more, and then left the church, together with the bearers of the bier, after he had ordered his servants to look after the philosopher and to take him back to the church after supper.

The coffin-bearers, when they returned to the house, all laid their hands on the stove. This custom is always observed in Little Russia by those who have seen a corpse.

The hunger which the philosopher now began to feel caused him for a while to forget the dead girl altogether. Gradually all the domestics of the house assembled in the kitchen; it was really a kind of club, where they were accustomed to gather. Even the dogs came to the door, wagging their tails in order to have bones and offal thrown to them.

If a servant was sent on an errand, he always found his way into the kitchen to rest there for a while, and to smoke a pipe. All the Cossacks of the establishment lay here during the whole day on and under the benches—in fact, wherever a place could be found to lie down in. Moreover, everyone was always leaving something behind in the kitchen—his cap, or his whip, or something of the sort. But the numbers of the club were not complete till the evening, when the groom came in after tying up his horses in the stable, the cowherd had shut up his cows in their stalls, and others collected there who were not usually seen in the day-time. During supper-time even the tongues of the laziest were set in motion. They talked of all and everything—of the new pair of breeches which someone had ordered for himself, of what might be in the centre of the earth, and of the wolf which someone had seen. There were a number of wits in the company—a class which is always represented in Little Russia.

The philosopher took his place with the rest in the great circle which sat round the kitchen door in the open-air. Soon an old woman with a red cap issued from it, bearing with both hands a large vessel full of hot "galuchkis," which she distributed among them. Each drew out of his pocket a wooden spoon, or a one-pronged wooden fork. As soon as their jaws began to move a little more slowly, and their wolfish hunger was somewhat appeased, they began to talk. The conversation, as might be expected, turned on the dead girl.

"Is it true," said a young shepherd, "is it true—though I cannot understand it—that our young mistress had traffic with evil spirits?"

"Who, the young lady?" answered Dorosch, whose acquaintance the philosopher had already made in the kibitka. "Yes, she was a regular witch! I can swear that she was a witch!"

"Hold your tongue, Dorosch!" exclaimed another—the one who, during the journey, had played the part of a consoler. "We have nothing to do with that. May God be merciful to her! One ought not to talk of such things."

But Dorosch was not at all inclined to be silent; he had just visited the wine-cellar with the steward on important business, and having stooped two or three times over one or two casks, he had returned in a very cheerful and loquacious mood.

"Why do you ask me to be silent?" he answered. "She has ridden on my own shoulders, I swear she has."

"Say, uncle," asked the young shepherd, "are there signs by which to recognise a sorceress?"

"No, there are not," answered Dorosch; "even if you knew the Psalter by heart, you could not recognise one."

"Yes, Dorosch, it is possible; don't talk such nonsense," retorted the former consoler. "It is not for nothing that God has given each some special peculiarity; the learned maintain that every witch has a little tail."

"Every old woman is a witch," said a grey-headed Cossack quite seriously.

"Yes, you are a fine lot," retorted the old woman who entered at that moment with a vessel full of fresh "galuchkis." "You are great fat pigs!"

A self-satisfied smile played round the lips of the old Cossack whose name was Javtuch, when he found that his remark had touched the old woman on a tender point. The shepherd burst into such a deep and loud explosion of laughter as if two oxen were lowing together.

This conversation excited in the philosopher a great curiosity, and a wish to obtain more exact information regarding the colonel's daughter. In order to lead the talk back to the subject, he turned to his next neighbour and said, "I should like to know why all the people here think that the young lady was a witch. Has she done harm to anyone, or killed them by witchcraft?"

"Yes, there are reports of that kind," answered a man, whose face was as flat as a shovel. "Who does not remember the huntsman Mikita, or the——"

"What has the huntsman Mikita got to do with it?" asked the philosopher.

"Stop; I will tell you the story of Mikita," interrupted Dorosch.

"No, I will tell it," said the groom, "for he was my godfather."

"I will tell the story of Mikita," said Spirid.

"Yes, yes, Spirid shall tell it," exclaimed the whole company; and Spirid began.

"You, Mr Philosopher Thomas, did not know Mikita. Ah! he was an extraordinary man. He knew every dog as though he were his own father. The present huntsman, Mikola, who sits three places away from me, is not fit to hold a candle to him, though good enough in his way; but compared to Mikita, he is a mere milksop."

"You tell the tale splendidly," exclaimed Dorosch, and nodded as a sign of approval.

Spirid continued.

"He saw a hare in the field quicker than you can take a pinch of snuff. He only needed to whistle 'Come here, Rasboy! Come here, Bosdraja!' and flew away on his horse like the wind, so that you could not say whether he went quicker than the dog or the dog than he. He could empty a quart pot of brandy in the twinkling of an eye. Ah! he was a splendid huntsman, only for some time he always had his eyes fixed on the young lady. Either he had fallen in love with her or she had bewitched him—in short, he went to the dogs. He became a regular old woman; yes, he became the devil knows what—it is not fitting to relate it."

"Very good," remarked Dorosch.

"If the young lady only looked at him, he let the reins slip out of his hands, called Bravko instead of Rasboy, stumbled, and made all kinds of mistakes. One day when he was currycombing a horse, the young lady came to him in the stable. 'Listen, Mikita,' she said. 'I should like for once to set my foot on you.' And he, the booby, was quite delighted, and answered, 'Don't only set your foot there, but sit on me altogether.' The young lady lifted her white little foot, and as soon as he saw it, his delight robbed him of his senses. He bowed his neck, the idiot, took her feet in both hands, and began to trot about like a horse all over the place. Whither they went he could not say; he returned more dead than alive, and from that time he wasted away and became as dry as a chip of wood. At last someone coming into the stable one day found instead of him only a handful of ashes and an empty jug; he had burned completely out. But it must be said he was a huntsman such as the world cannot match."

When Spirid had ended his tale, they all began to vie with one another in praising the deceased huntsman.

"And have you heard the story of Cheptchicha?" asked Dorosch, turning to Thomas.

"No."

"Ha! Ha! One sees they don't teach you much in your seminary. Well, listen. We have here in our village a Cossack called Cheptoun, a fine fellow. Sometimes indeed he amuses himself by stealing and lying without any reason; but he is a fine fellow for all that. His house is not far away from here. One evening, just about this time, Cheptoun and his wife went to bed after they had finished their day's work. Since it was fine weather, Cheptchicha went to sleep in the court-yard, and Cheptoun in the house—no! I mean Cheptchicha went to sleep in the house on a bench and Cheptoun outside——"

"No, Cheptchicha didn't go to sleep on a bench, but on the ground," interrupted the old woman who stood at the door.

Dorosch looked at her, then at the ground, then again at her, and said after a pause, "If I tore your dress off your back before all these people, it wouldn't look pretty."

The rebuke was effectual. The old woman was silent, and did not interrupt again.

Dorosch continued.

"In the cradle which hung in the middle of the room lay a one-year-old child. I do not know whether it was a boy or a girl. Cheptchicha had lain down, and heard on the other side of the door a dog scratching and howling loud enough to frighten anyone. She was afraid, for women are such simple folk that if one puts out one's tongue at them behind the door in the dark, their hearts sink into their boots. 'But,' she thought to herself, 'I must give this cursed dog one on the snout to stop his howling!' So she seized the poker and opened the door. But hardly had she done so than the dog rushed between her legs straight to the cradle. Then Cheptchicha saw that it was not a dog but the young lady; and if it had only been the young lady as she knew her it wouldn't have mattered, but she looked quite blue, and her eyes sparkled like fiery coals. She seized the child, bit its throat, and began to suck its blood. Cheptchicha shrieked, 'Ah! my darling child!' and rushed out of the room. Then she saw that the house-door was shut and rushed up to the attic and sat there, the stupid woman, trembling all over. Then the young lady came after her and bit her too, poor fool! The next morning Cheptoun carried his wife, all bitten and wounded, down from the attic, and the next day she died. Such strange things happen in the world. One may wear fine clothes, but that does not matter; a witch is and remains a witch."

After telling his story, Dorosch looked around him with a complacent air, and cleaned out his pipe with his little finger in order to fill it again. The story of the witch had made a deep impression on all, and each of them had something to say about her. One had seen her come to the door of his house in the form of a hayrick; from others she had stolen their caps or their pipes; she had cut off the hair-plaits of many girls in the village, and drunk whole pints of the blood of others.

At last the whole company observed that they had gossiped over their time, for it was already night. All looked for a sleeping place—some in the kitchen and others in the barn or the court-yard.

"Now, Mr Thomas, it is time that we go to the dead," said the grey-headed Cossack, turning to the philosopher. All four—Spirid, Dorosch, the old Cossack, and the philosopher—betook themselves to the church, keeping off with their whips the wild dogs who roamed about the roads in great numbers and bit the sticks of passers-by in sheer malice.

Although the philosopher had seized the opportunity of fortifying himself beforehand with a stiff glass of brandy, yet he felt a certain secret fear which increased as he approached the church, which was lit up within. The strange tales he had heard had made a deep impression on his imagination. They had passed the thick hedges and trees, and the country became more open. At last they reached the small enclosure round the church; behind it there were no more trees, but a huge, empty plain dimly visible in the darkness. The three Cossacks ascended the steep steps with Thomas, and entered the church. Here they left the philosopher, expressing their hope that he would successfully accomplish his duties, and locked him in as their master had ordered.

He was left alone. At first he yawned, then he stretched himself, blew on both hands, and finally looked round him. In the middle of the church stood the black bier; before the dark pictures of saints burned the candles, whose light only illuminated the icons, and cast a faint glimmer into the body of the church; all the corners were in complete darkness. The lofty icons seemed to be of considerable age; only a little of the original gilt remained on their broken traceries; the faces of the saints had become quite black and looked uncanny.

Once more the philosopher cast a glance around him. "Bother it!" said he to himself. "What is there to be afraid about? No living creature can get in, and as for the dead and those who come from the 'other side,' I can protect myself with such effectual prayers that they cannot touch me with the tips of their fingers. There is nothing to fear," he repeated, swinging his arms. "Let us begin the prayers!"

As he approached one of the side-aisles, he noticed two packets of candles which had been placed there.

"That is fine," he thought. "I must illuminate the whole church, till it is as bright as day. What a pity that one cannot smoke in it."

He began to light the candles on all the wall-brackets and all the candelabra, as well as those already burning before the holy pictures; soon the whole church was brilliantly lit up. Only the darkness in the roof above seemed still denser by contrast, and the faces of the saints peering out of the frames looked as unearthly as before. He approached the bier, looked nervously at the face of the dead girl, could not help shuddering slightly, and involuntarily closed his eyes. What terrible and extraordinary beauty!

He turned away and tried to go to one side, but the strange curiosity and peculiar fascination which men feel in moments of fear, compelled him to look again and again, though with a similar shudder. And in truth there was something terrible about the beauty of the dead girl. Perhaps she would not have inspired so much fear had she been less beautiful; but there was nothing ghastly or deathlike in the face, which wore rather an expression of life, and it seemed to the philosopher as though she were watching him from under her closed eyelids. He even thought he saw a tear roll from under the eyelash of her right eye, but when it was halfway down her cheek, he saw that it was a drop of blood.

He quickly went into one of the stalls, opened his book, and began to read the prayers in a very loud voice in order to keep up his courage. His deep voice sounded strange to himself in the grave-like silence; it aroused no echo in the silent and desolate wooden walls of the church.

"What is there to be afraid of?" he thought to himself. "She will not rise from her bier, since she fears God's word. She will remain quietly resting. Yes, and what sort of a Cossack should I be, if I were afraid? The fact is, I have drunk a little too much—that is why I feel so queer. Let me take a pinch of snuff. It is really excellent—first-rate!"

At the same time he cast a furtive glance over the pages of the prayer-book towards the bier, and involuntarily he said to himself, "There! See! She is getting up! Her head is already above the edge of the coffin!"

But a death-like silence prevailed; the coffin was motionless, and all the candles shone steadily. It was an awe-inspiring sight, this church lit up at midnight, with the corpse in the midst, and no living soul near but one. The philosopher began to sing in various keys in order to stifle his fears, but every moment he glanced across at the coffin, and involuntarily the question came to his lips, "Suppose she rose up after all?"

But the coffin did not move. Nowhere was there the slightest sound nor stir. Not even did a cricket chirp in any corner. There was nothing audible but the slight sputtering of some distant candle, or the faint fall of a drop of wax.

"Suppose she rose up after all?"

He raised his head. Then he looked round him wildly and rubbed his eyes. Yes, she was no longer lying in the coffin, but sitting upright. He turned away his eyes, but at once looked again, terrified, at the coffin. She stood up; then she walked with closed eyes through the church, stretching out her arms as though she wanted to seize someone.

She now came straight towards him. Full of alarm, he traced with his finger a circle round himself; then in a loud voice he began to recite the prayers and formulas of exorcism which he had learnt from a monk who had often seen witches and evil spirits.

She had almost reached the edge of the circle which he had traced; but it was evident that she had not the power to enter it. Her face wore a bluish tint like that of one who has been several days dead.

Thomas had not the courage to look at her, so terrible was her appearance; her teeth chattered and she opened her dead eyes, but as in her rage she saw nothing, she turned in another direction and felt with outstretched arms among the pillars and corners of the church in the hope of seizing him.

At last she stood still, made a threatening gesture, and then lay down again in the coffin.

The philosopher could not recover his self-possession, and kept on gazing anxiously at it. Suddenly it rose from its place and began hurtling about the church with a whizzing sound. At one time it was almost directly over his head; but the philosopher observed that it could not pass over the area of his charmed circle, so he kept on repeating his formulas of exorcism. The coffin now fell with a crash in the middle of the church, and remained lying there motionless. The corpse rose again; it had now a greenish-blue colour, but at the same moment the distant crowing of a cock was audible, and it lay down again.

The philosopher's heart beat violently, and the perspiration poured in streams from his face; but heartened by the crowing of the cock, he rapidly repeated the prayers.

As the first light of dawn looked through the windows, there came a deacon and the grey-haired Javtuk, who acted as sacristan, in order to release him. When he had reached the house, he could not sleep for a long time; but at last weariness overpowered him, and he slept till noon. When he awoke, his experiences of the night appeared to him like a dream. He was given a quart of brandy to strengthen him.

At table he was again talkative and ate a fairly large sucking pig almost without assistance. But none the less he resolved to say nothing of what he had seen, and to all curious questions only returned the answer, "Yes, some wonderful things happened."

The philosopher was one of those men who, when they have had a good meal, are uncommonly amiable. He lay down on a bench, with his pipe in his mouth, looked blandly at all, and expectorated every minute.

But as the evening approached, he became more and more pensive. About supper-time nearly the whole company had assembled in order to play "krapli." This is a kind of game of skittles, in which, instead of bowls, long staves are used, and the winner has the right to ride on the back of his opponent. It provided the spectators with much amusement; sometimes the groom, a huge man, would clamber on the back of the swineherd, who was slim and short and shrunken; another time the groom would present his own back, while Dorosch sprang on it shouting, "What a regular ox!" Those of the company who were more staid sat by the threshold of the kitchen. They looked uncommonly serious, smoked their pipes, and did not even smile when the younger ones went into fits of laughter over some joke of the groom or Spirid.

Thomas vainly attempted to take part in the game; a gloomy thought was firmly fixed like a nail in his head. In spite of his desperate efforts to appear cheerful after supper, fear had overmastered his whole being, and it increased with the growing darkness.

"Now it is time for us to go, Mr Student!" said the grey-haired Cossack, and stood up with Dorosch. "Let us betake ourselves to our work."

Thomas was conducted to the church in the same way as on the previous evening; again he was left alone, and the door was bolted behind him.

As soon as he found himself alone, he began to feel in the grip of his fears. He again saw the dark pictures of the saints in their gilt frames, and the black coffin, which stood menacing and silent in the middle of the church.

"Never mind!" he said to himself. "I am over the first shock. The first time I was frightened, but I am not so at all now—no, not at all!"

He quickly went into a stall, drew a circle round him with his finger, uttered some prayers and formulas for exorcism, and then began to read the prayers for the dead in a loud voice and with the fixed resolution not to look up from the book nor take notice of anything.

He did so for an hour, and began to grow a little tired; he cleared his throat and drew his snuff-box out of his pocket, but before he had taken a pinch he looked nervously towards the coffin.

A sudden chill shot through him. The witch was already standing before him on the edge of the circle, and had fastened her green eyes upon him. He shuddered, looked down at the book, and began to read his prayers and exorcisms aloud. Yet all the while he was aware how her teeth chattered, and how she stretched out her arms to seize him. But when he cast a hasty glance towards her, he saw that she was not looking in his direction, and it was clear that she could not see him.

Then she began to murmur in an undertone, and terrible words escaped her lips—words that sounded like the bubbling of boiling pitch. The philosopher did not know their meaning, but he knew that they signified something terrible, and were intended to counteract his exorcisms.

After she had spoken, a stormy wind arose in the church, and there was a noise like the rushing of many birds. He heard the noise of their wings and claws as they flapped against and scratched at the iron bars of the church windows. There were also violent blows on the church door, as if someone were trying to break it in pieces.

The philosopher's heart beat violently; he did not dare to look up, but continued to read the prayers without a pause. At last there was heard in the distance the shrill sound of a cock's crow. The exhausted philosopher stopped and gave a great sigh of relief.

Those who came to release him found him more dead than alive; he had leant his back against the wall, and stood motionless, regarding them without any expression in his eyes. They were obliged almost to carry him to the house; he then shook himself, asked for and drank a quart of brandy. He passed his hand through his hair and said, "There are all sorts of horrors in the world, and such dreadful things happen that——" Here he made a gesture as though to ward off something. All who heard him bent their heads forward in curiosity. Even a small boy, who ran on everyone's errands, stood by with his mouth wide open.

Just then a young woman in a close-fitting dress passed by. She was the old cook's assistant, and very coquettish; she always stuck something in her bodice by way of ornament, a ribbon or a flower, or even a piece of paper if she could find nothing else.

"Good day, Thomas," she said, as she saw the philosopher. "Dear me! what has happened to you?" she exclaimed, striking her hands together.

"Well, what is it, you silly creature?"

"Good heavens! You have grown quite grey!"

"Yes, so he has!" said Spirid, regarding him more closely. "You have grown as grey as our old Javtuk."

When the philosopher heard that, he hastened into the kitchen, where he had noticed on the wall a dirty, three-cornered piece of looking-glass. In front of it hung some forget-me-nots, evergreens, and a small garland—a proof that it was the toilette-glass of the young coquette. With alarm he saw that it actually was as they had said—his hair was quite grizzled.

He sank into a reverie; at last he said to himself, "I will go to the colonel, tell him all, and declare that I will read no more prayers. He must send me back at once to Kieff." With this intention he turned towards the door-steps of the colonel's house.

The colonel was sitting motionless in his room; his face displayed the same hopeless grief which Thomas had observed on it on his first arrival, only the hollows in his cheeks had deepened. It was obvious that he took very little or no food. A strange paleness made him look almost as though made of marble.

"Good day," he said as he observed Thomas standing, cap in hand, at the door. "Well, how are you getting on? All right?"

"Yes, sir, all right! Such hellish things are going on, that one would like to rush away as far as one's feet can carry one."

"How so?"

"Your daughter, sir…. When one considers the matter, she is, of course, of noble descent—no one can dispute that; but don't be angry, and may God grant her eternal rest!"

"Very well! What about her?"

"She is in league with the devil. She inspires one with such dread that all prayers are useless."

"Pray! Pray! It was not for nothing that she sent for you. My dove was troubled about her salvation, and wished to expel all evil influences by means of prayer."

"I swear, gracious sir, it is beyond my power."

"Pray! Pray!" continued the colonel in the same persuasive tone. "There is only one night more; you are doing a Christian work, and I will reward you richly."

"However great your rewards may be, I will not read the prayers any more, sir," said Thomas in a tone of decision.

"Listen, philosopher!" said the colonel with a menacing air. "I will not allow any objections. In your seminary you may act as you like, but here it won't do. If I have you knouted, it will be somewhat different to the rector's canings. Do you know what a strong 'kantchuk'(2) is?"

"Of course I do," said the philosopher in a low voice; "a number of them together are insupportable."

"Yes, I think so too. But you don't know yet how hot my fellows can make it," replied the colonel threateningly. He sprang up, and his face assumed a fierce, despotic expression, betraying the savagery of his nature, which had been only temporarily modified by grief. "After the first flogging they pour on brandy and then repeat it. Go away and finish your work. If you don't obey, you won't be able to stand again, and if you do, you will get a thousand ducats."

"That is a devil of a fellow," thought the philosopher to himself, and went out. "One can't trifle with him. But wait a little, my friend; I will escape you so cleverly, that even your hounds can't find me!"

He determined, under any circumstances, to run away, and only waited till the hour after dinner arrived, when all the servants were accustomed to take a nap on the hay in the barn, and to snore and puff so loudly that it sounded as if machinery had been set up there. At last the time came. Even Javtuch stretched himself out in the sun and closed his eyes. Tremblingly, and on tiptoe, the philosopher stole softly into the garden, whence he thought he could escape more easily into the open country. This garden was generally so choked up with weeds that it seemed admirably adapted for such an attempt. With the exception of a single path used by the people of the house, the whole of it was covered with cherry-trees, elder-bushes, and tall heath-thistles with fibrous red buds. All these trees and bushes had been thickly overgrown with ivy, which formed a kind of roof. Its tendrils reached to the hedge and fell down on the other side in snake-like curves among the small, wild field-flowers. Behind the hedge which bordered the garden was a dense mass of wild heather, in which it did not seem probable that anyone would care to venture himself, and the strong, stubborn stems of which seemed likely to baffle any attempt to cut them.

As the philosopher was about to climb over the hedge, his teeth chattered, and his heart beat so violently that he felt frightened at it. The skirts of his long cloak seemed to cling to the ground as though they had been fastened to it by pegs. When he had actually got over the hedge he seemed to hear a shrill voice crying behind him "Whither? Whither?"

He jumped into the heather and began to run, stumbling over old roots and treading on unfortunate moles. When he had emerged from the heather he saw that he still had a wide field to cross, behind which was a thick, thorny underwood. This, according to his calculation, must stretch as far as the road leading to Kieff, and if he reached it he would be safe. Accordingly he ran over the field and plunged into the thorny copse. Every sharp thorn he encountered tore a fragment from his coat. Then he reached a small open space; in the centre of it stood a willow, whose branches hung down to the earth, and close by flowed a clear spring bright as silver. The first thing the philosopher did was to lie down and drink eagerly, for he was intolerably thirsty.

"Splendid water!" he said, wiping his mouth. "This is a good place to rest in."

"No, better run farther; perhaps we are being followed," said a voice immediately behind him.

Thomas started and turned; before him stood Javtuch.

"This devil of a Javtuch!" he thought. "I should like to seize him by the feet and smash his hang-dog face against the trunk of a tree."

"Why did you go round such a long way?" continued Javtuch. "You had much better have chosen the path by which I came; it leads directly by the stable. Besides, it is a pity about your coat. Such splendid cloth! How much did it cost an ell? Well, we have had a long enough walk; it is time to go home."

The philosopher followed Javtuch in a very depressed state.

"Now the accursed witch will attack me in earnest," he thought. "But what have I really to fear? Am I not a Cossack? I have read the prayers for two nights already; with God's help I will get through the third night also. It is plain that the witch must have a terrible load of guilt upon her, else the evil one would not help her so much."

Feeling somewhat encouraged by these reflections, he returned to the court-yard and asked Dorosch, who sometimes, by the steward's permission, had access to the wine-cellar, to fetch him a small bottle of brandy. The two friends sat down before a barn and drank a pretty large one. Suddenly the philosopher jumped up and said, "I want musicians! Bring some musicians!"

But without waiting for them he began to dance the "tropak" in the court-yard. He danced till tea-time, and the servants, who, as is usual in such cases, had formed a small circle round him, grew at last tired of watching him, and went away saying, "By heavens, the man can dance!"

Finally the philosopher lay down in the place where he had been dancing, and fell asleep. It was necessary to pour a bucket of cold water on his head to wake him up for supper. At the meal he enlarged on the topic of what a Cossack ought to be, and how he should not be afraid of anything in the world.

"It is time," said Javtuch; "let us go."

"I wish I could put a lighted match to your tongue," thought the philosopher; then he stood up and said, "Let us go."

On their way to the church, the philosopher kept looking round him on all sides, and tried to start a conversation with his companions; but both Javtuch and Dorosch remained silent. It was a weird night. In the distance wolves howled continually, and even the barking of the dogs had something unearthly about it.

"That doesn't sound like wolves howling, but something else," remarked Dorosch.

Javtuch still kept silence, and the philosopher did not know what answer to make.

They reached the church and walked over the old wooden planks, whose rotten condition showed how little the lord of the manor cared about God and his soul. Javtuch and Dorosch left the philosopher alone, as on the previous evenings.

There was still the same atmosphere of menacing silence in the church, in the centre of which stood the coffin with the terrible witch inside it.

"I am not afraid, by heavens, I am not afraid!" he said; and after drawing a circle round himself as before, he began to read the prayers and exorcisms.

An oppressive silence prevailed; the flickering candles filled the church with their clear light. The philosopher turned one page after another, and noticed that he was not reading what was in the book. Full of alarm, he crossed himself and began to sing a hymn. This calmed him somewhat, and he resumed his reading, turning the pages rapidly as he did so.

Suddenly in the midst of the sepulchral silence the iron lid of the coffin sprang open with a jarring noise, and the dead witch stood up. She was this time still more terrible in aspect than at first. Her teeth chattered loudly and her lips, through which poured a stream of dreadful curses, moved convulsively. A whirlwind arose in the church; the icons of the saints fell on the ground, together with the broken window-panes. The door was wrenched from its hinges, and a huge mass of monstrous creatures rushed into the church, which became filled with the noise of beating wings and scratching claws. All these creatures flew and crept about, seeking for the philosopher, from whose brain the last fumes of intoxication had vanished. He crossed himself ceaselessly and uttered prayer after prayer, hearing all the time the whole unclean swarm rustling about him, and brushing him with the tips of their wings. He had not the courage to look at them; he only saw one uncouth monster standing by the wall, with long, shaggy hair and two flaming eyes. Over him something hung in the air which looked like a gigantic bladder covered with countless crabs' claws and scorpions' stings, and with black clods of earth hanging from it. All these monsters stared about seeking him, but they could not find him, since he was protected by his sacred circle.

"Bring the Viy(3)! Bring the Viy!" cried the witch.

A sudden silence followed; the howling of wolves was heard in the distance, and soon heavy footsteps resounded through the church. Thomas looked up furtively and saw that an ungainly human figure with crooked legs was being led into the church. He was quite covered with black soil, and his hands and feet resembled knotted roots. He trod heavily and stumbled at every step. His eyelids were of enormous length. With terror, Thomas saw that his face was of iron. They led him in by the arms and placed him near Thomas's circle.

"Raise my eyelids! I can't see anything!" said the Viy in a dull, hollow voice, and they all hastened to help in doing so.

"Don't look!" an inner voice warned the philosopher; but he could not restrain from looking.

"There he is!" exclaimed the Viy, pointing an iron finger at him; and all the monsters rushed on him at once.

Struck dumb with terror, he sank to the ground and died.

At that moment there sounded a cock's crow for the second time; the earth-spirits had not heard the first one. In alarm they hurried to the windows and the door to get out as quickly as possible. But it was too late; they all remained hanging as though fastened to the door and the windows.

When the priest came he stood amazed at such a desecration of God's house, and did not venture to read prayers there. The church remained standing as it was, with the monsters hanging on the windows and the door. Gradually it became overgrown with creepers, bushes, and wild heather, and no one can discover it now.

. . . . . .

When the report of this event reached Kieff, and the theologian Khalava heard what a fate had overtaken the philosopher Thomas, he sank for a whole hour into deep reflection. He had greatly altered of late; after finishing his studies he had become bell-ringer of one of the chief churches in the city, and he always appeared with a bruised nose, because the belfry staircase was in a ruinous condition.

"Have you heard what has happened to Thomas?" said Tiberius Gorobetz, who had become a philosopher and now wore a moustache.

"Yes; God had appointed it so," answered the bell-ringer. "Let us go to the ale-house; we will drink a glass to his memory."

The young philosopher, who, with the enthusiasm of a novice, had made such full use of his privileges as a student that his breeches and coat and even his cap reeked of brandy and tobacco, agreed readily to the proposal.

"He was a fine fellow, Thomas," said the bell-ringer as the limping innkeeper set the third jug of beer before him. "A splendid fellow! And lost his life for nothing!"

"I know why he perished," said Gorobetz; "because he was afraid. If he had not feared her, the witch could have done nothing to him. One ought to cross oneself incessantly and spit exactly on her tail, and then not the least harm can happen. I know all about it, for here, in Kieff, all the old women in the market-place are witches."

The bell-ringer nodded assent. But being aware that he could not say any more, he got up cautiously and went out, swaying to the right and left in order to find a hiding-place in the thick steppe grass outside the town. At the same time, in accordance with his old habits, he did not forget to steal an old boot-sole which lay on the ale-house bench.

THE END